Melanie Ifield

Listening
to Echoes of her Self

A Melanie Ifield book
First published by Melanie Ifield in 2015
Copyright © Melanie Ifield 2015
ISBN: 978-0-9922839-7-1

Cover art image Copyright ©: Olga LIS (www.bigstockphotos.com)
Cover arranged by: Shane Seczkowski
Typeset & formatting: Thomas White
All rights reserved
www.melanieifield.com

Author: Ifield, Melanie
Title: Listening to Echoes of her Self / Melanie Ifield
Target audience: Adults

Books published by Melanie Ifield

Listening to Echoes of her Self

PART I: AT THE END- A LIFETIME AWAY

Finding the moment

The world is walking backwards, she thought, watching two men arguing about a taxi fare outside her window. She took another sip of her hot tea.

As far as she could tell, admittedly from a rather limited point of view (she was the first to admit that a purely personal view point tended to limit one's scope for the fullness of things), the world kept looking back for the answers to the future. People all around her kept one wary eye over their shoulder, lest the past slip up and grab them; instead of keeping both eyes on the path in front of them.

'It leads to most of them tripping over their own feet,' she said out loud, just to hear something other than the two men.

One was the taxi driver. The other was the fare. She didn't see what the fuss was about. The man was too lazy to walk, couldn't walk, or had no other means of getting around. Neither she nor the taxi driver cared. Either way, he owed what he owed. Such was life.

She looked over at the pile of newspapers in the corner to distract herself from the continued unpleasantness outside. She firmly believed that some people didn't realise how much toxic energy they leaked out all over the place. And all over other people while they were at it.

One day, she thought, she'd stop her order of the newspapers. She'd stopped reading them months ago: every day, the same old garbage. Toxic people doing toxic things worried about the opinion of others. Governments inventing conspiracies and Great Fears (to perpetuate the 'us and them' feeling in the world), and offering succour to the frightened; afraid that the people might think for themselves. Only they never appeared to do so. They accepted whatever was said, whatever the news told them was happening and sat in lines on Sunday, their bottoms going numb on hardened benches, allowing someone else to tell them what to think and how to feel about the forever that faced them once their bodies gave up.

Putting down the tea she stood up and stretched. She hadn't been to church in so many years she'd lost count. One day, it had all seemed highly irrelevant to her life. A dusty old man telling dusty old stories, chosen by men long since dust themselves. Once she'd learned the Bible had been put together by a Council of Men, picking over what stories they wished to keep and those they wished to consign to history, she'd given up. Seeing as most people tended to lie so the facts suited their point of view, she had chosen to stop believing in everything she read or heard from others. She listened to herself. This caused all sorts of problems.

'The thing is, Socrates, people have stopped listening to themselves. It's called insane to talk to your Self, though if anyone listened, they would realise that the only person who ever really knows them and has all the answers, is the Self.' She stroked her cat, the magical Socrates, a Siamese who had a lot to say about everything, even at nearly twenty years of age.

Socrates was actually a de-sexed female cat, but she hadn't realised that until she took her in for the operation. It had come as a magical surprise. She had suddenly discovered it was okay to believe what Socrates had to say; he was after all, a woman. The only trouble was Socrates refused to respond to any other name. So Socrates he/she remained. It was confusing to guests. So she stopped having guests. At least, that was the reason she gave to herself. The fact was she no longer knew enough people close enough to her to bother. If she had a party, it would be a small one. Like the one she'd planned for her ninetieth.

There was the lady down at the end of the street who talked to her washing line and sometimes the pegs. She often went into hospital because the fairies in her garden wouldn't keep the noise down after dark. She knew exactly how that woman felt. She was too tired to listen anymore, too.

People still turned up at her doorstep asking for help. They had lost someone they loved, or couldn't find their favourite toy. One person turned up because her daughter wasn't sleeping. In the end she discovered a frisky kitten was coming to visit at midnight and keeping the child awake to play. Nobody liked to be alone at midnight. Not even spirits. Not if they were little and scared. She'd invited it to come home with her and now the kitten played with Socrates; who had taught it some manners about midnight jaunts. Socrates wasn't up for nightly playing. She was too old for all that rubbish.

She looked out over the tops of trees and into the hills behind the city. For years she'd worked hard and fitted in. As payment, she had a lovely home, with views many would kill for. She should know. People had killed for less and she held witness to it when distraught relatives came to her wanting to know why.

In those days, she'd cared enough to have the answers. She'd been one open heart of caring.

'Every one of them,' she'd told a friend. 'I can't tell the difference. I love them all. When I am with a person, they are the only person in the world to me. I give them all of me.'

And it had been true; until it wasn't.

Many years ago, someone had said to her that her gift was making the person she was with feel as though they were the most important person in the world. And everything they said was of vital importance.

When she was with someone, they became the centre of her Universe. They had her undivided attention. Everything they said was fascinating and she was moved. She felt that she couldn't possibly care about another as much as she cared about that one person and their burning issue.

They had all of her; until they didn't.

She'd leave their company and start to talk to another, and suddenly, it was as if that person was the most fascinating she'd ever met...

It led to some confusion. People didn't realise she could feel that way about everyone without diminishing how she felt about them. She felt she had enough love inside her to power the world. And she fell in love with the stories of nearly everyone she met. Though they didn't understand this simple truth:

'Everyone is fascinating in their own unique way'.

She learned that from a tree.

It was strange how that kept popping into her mind lately.

Everyone had something in their heart they wished that someone would stop and hear. Everyone waited for that certain someone to come along, fill their hearts with meaning, and listen. They even wanted that person to care. Except when that person came along, living their stories alongside the other and loving them because of their stories, they wanted that person to be theirs and theirs alone. They also wanted them to listen only to *them*.

The human condition, she supposed. Humans didn't seem to like to share affection. Man wouldn't share woman; woman fought over man. Husbands grew jealous over the love wives had for their children; and women complained bitterly about golf, fishing and football.

They'd learned to keep their hearts small. From the very beginning, it was a battle to stay as small as possible. Don't allow the world to see me, they cried to one another. They might see the flaws, the imperfections, the lies, the guilt. She'd heard it all. People thought they were covering it up. They were just burying it under a concrete layer of civility; until that crumbled and they took to the neighbour's wife with a hatchet. Sometimes it was themselves they destroyed.

Under the layers of concrete they had made, the truth was something burning to shine itself free. And no matter what people did, in the end, it would.

She supposed it was the reason there were so many distorted realities floating about. People had forgotten how to shine and the cracks in the concrete only allowed glimpses of what could be, so they were running around wearing motley: patches of black and glimpses of light. It made for a right mess in the head.

The panacea for all problems was now to go to the doctor and not even try to uncover themselves. There was always the chance that by doing so, they might end up naked: stripped to the bare essentials. She wondered why it took extreme measures in many cases to crack the civility and render the person in their full colour, if it was ever seen at all.

She'd come to the conclusion she wasn't strictly normal the first time she'd talked to a tree. It wasn't the talking to the tree itself that had caused her to ponder her own position. That was not so remarkable. People talked to themselves, or things around them, all the time. Nobody appeared to care about that. They smiled and nodded, agreeing that it was eccentric, but muttering when shopping/washing/cooking was allowed.

The tree responding was when she decided something needed to be done with her life. It had surprised her no end that she could hear such a thing.

It had happened after a protracted bout of flu. She'd been happily hallucinating after too many days of dehydration and possibly a chest infection, and this had allowed the mental barriers to slide away. Once that was discarded, she was able to do many things she'd never tried before. Casting aside the trappings of civilisation had been remarkably freeing. Luckily she'd had a private garden. No one could see, or mind, the strange naked lady wandering from tree to flower, communing with colours she hadn't even known were there.

This then, she had realised, was what it must be like to take a trip. She'd never done drugs, always thinking that the lack of control would lead to disaster. But as she wandered her garden back then, she'd wished she'd been gamer when she was younger. Not that, at the grand age of thirty, she was considered old. But she certainly had a few more miles on the clock and the idea of indulging in drugs at thirty seemed – negligent for some reason.

Looking back at this memory from closer to ninety, she had to smile. Thirty had seemed old. Well, not so much old, as settled: settled into shape, into patterns, into the living of a life. It had taken the flu to make her realise she hadn't been living at all.

That the restlessness, the feeling that her life didn't fit and that something was wrong, wasn't so strange, after all. She'd often tried to catch that elusive thought, or turned her head because there'd been a whisper she'd failed to hear. There had been hints and feelings that this wasn't living – it was merely existing.

With civilisation relegated to the back of her mind, she was free to sense things about herself she had never known to be true. One of these things was she was a very magical being indeed.

As were the rest of them – all the people around her she had tried to block out, but humanity seemed to stink of such rich layers of fear, corruption and excitement, it had lost the scent of magical innocence.

They covered themselves in expectation and past failure, as though those two things would somehow lead to a better outcome. There were so many rules to make sure that no one was responsible for anything, she didn't see how anyone could cope getting out of bed in the morning. They might stub a toe and have to call the Council to remove their rug; then sue the rug people because it hadn't come with a warning label to explain that sudden movements, if the rug was bunched up, might lead to toe damage. These things had to be considered.

She had sat down next to the tree in question and leaned back on it, resting her head against the enormous trunk. The smooth bark was cool against her hair and she could see all the way up into the top most branches waving above her. It had made a lovely sighing sound and this had comforted her.

Leaning there, she had asked why it was she felt so dissatisfied with life. Her life, just to be exact; she wasn't overly concerned with those around her at that point. They seemed to be as joyless and as routinised as her, but that wasn't her concern. There had to be something missing; only she didn't know what it was or how to get it. She'd been searching around, putting her finger in many pies, wishing that one of them felt 'right'. None of them had.

They'd all been variations on the same theme, had been the trouble. There was nothing new or exciting. She'd left the dreaming to the young girl she hadn't been for many years. That young girl had talked to many things, most of them unseen to the naked adult eye. She had dreamed and laughed and skipped about waving her arms, like the branches overhead. But way before thirty, she'd squashed any dreaming. It wasn't allowed in the adult world. Dreams came under the heading of immaturity and adults were meant to be full of responsibility. Some of them even had the responsibilities to go with all that fullness.

But somehow, this adult world with its fullness and self importance, only left her feeling confused and out of touch. Like she was hurtling along out of control, while pretending she had the steering wheel in her hands and she was fine. It didn't matter that she was headed towards a massive crater in the road, thank you: She could manage.

Did they all feel this way, she wondered? Slightly off centre, with the foot hovering halfway between the accelerator and the brake pedal, hoping they'd make the right decision at the last second.

She'd been naked, under a tree, coming out of the flu. The hallucinogenic qualities she'd discovered from the flu had worn off and she was exhausted. Cool, but it had been a lovely spring day, so she wasn't too cold. She leaned against that tree and stared vaguely up at the heavens, as though accusing God of not knowing what She was about.

Who would send a bunch of children to rule the world? Because if truth was told and she had lost any interest in lying to herself, she'd met very few adults running around the world. When she looked about, at the scheming women, the competitive men, the preening and gloating that went on around her at work, it just looked like the playground of a rather badly unkempt high school – only much, much more sinister.

These people had power.

Thinking about the past had made her hungry. At ninety, her appetite had diminished so much; it was a relief to feel hungry at all.

She scratched Socrates between the ears, which earned her a growl. If there was something Socrates hated, it was to be scratched when she hadn't asked for it. But since Socrates rarely did, it left her with no alternative but to steal a scratch while the damned cat wasn't looking. Socrates growled a low warning rumble in the back of her throat.

'Well, I don't remember asking for your opinion. It was just a friendly scratch, more of a hello really. I can't believe I'm been told off for being friendly,' she informed the cat, who sniffed in a very dignified manner.

'True, I can see your point. I'd hate it if someone was overly familiar with me in such a way without my permission. I apologise. Perhaps we could resume my rather disjointed trip down memory lane? Would that be okay with you?'

She left the family room, misnamed by the realtor who sold her the place, seeing as she had no family. Well, nothing that wasn't four legged, or crystalline. Placing her cup in the sink, she took out last night's leftovers and found herself a fork.

The trouble with living alone was it was all too easy to fall into bad habits. She could eat the same meals over and over, pretending that she didn't mind, that variety wasn't her spice of life; when in fact, she'd have loved something new and tasty, only couldn't be bothered. It also meant she could eat whenever she pleased. There were no timetables. No need to put meals on tables at certain hours, just her own stomach, marching to its own beat, telling her when it was hungry. The fact she'd missed lunch because breakfast hadn't been until eleven thirty might have contributed.

She took the bowl of leftovers and the fork into the office. There were things she had to write, notes to type up. If she was ever to write it all down, she would have to get her act together. Time wasn't on her side. Not anymore.

At one point the years had stretched out – an endless repetitious reminder that she hadn't achieved everything she had set her teenage heart on. Now – they were running away like a locomotive: pounding down the days and hours. She could see the tunnel, even if it was still some distance away.

Not that long ago she'd been sixty. Things had appeared to suddenly come into rather clear focus. Time wasn't on anyone's side when they were sixty, she had thought vaguely. Sixty was only the new fifty for those who could be bothered with botox, collagen and fashion. Her wardrobe was a series of white or violet flowing tops, pants or dresses. Shapelessness had come to appeal when her hips no longer looked flattering in jeans and a flat chest was no longer something that enabled her to look like a good athlete (not that she had ever attempted to be a good athlete, but at least she looked as though it was possible). People just saw bony shoulders, flat top and lumpy thighs. Now they saw nothing.

It was with her underwear that colours could shine. Everyone was allowed one vanity. Pretty colours close to the skin was hers.

She shifted aside sheets of paper, uncovering a laptop. It was one concession to technology she allowed herself. There were no TVs, no radios, no mobile phones, iPods or dishwasher in her house. But the laptop was a must. There were too many words left inside to leave it to the chancy writing of her tired hands. She'd had to put aside the flowing script of calligraphy, pen and paper, years ago.

Socrates made her way into the room, sniffing the air and making nice noises.

'You want some of this, don't you?' She smiled rather grimly, waving the forkful of chicken risotto in Socrates' direction. 'I have something you want, so suddenly you'll be nice to me. Typical cat.'

She said this with great affection and not an ounce of truth. Every cat owner (or any human owned by a cat) knew the language of their cat. There was nothing typical about them. Personality wise, they were deeper and more real than any human, she had discovered. Cats were all about the Now. They didn't require people to service their needs; they did exactly what they wanted when the mood struck them. Humans, she decided, could learn quite a lot about life studying cats.

Socrates understood the deficiencies of humanity. She was

constantly telling her human about them. They didn't always agree, but it made for some very interesting conversations nonetheless.

Right now, Socrates didn't just want the food. She wanted her human to keep remembering. It was important that all of her memories were spelled out. Socrates would always listen.

They shared some late lunch and the laptop was opened. That was as far as things went. She was distracted a lot lately. It was hard to keep her mind flowing in one direction. She looked fondly at Socrates.

'I'm getting as bad as my neighbours. Looking backwards so far, I forget how to live in the moment and muddle up my feet.'

Socrates just purred, licking her front paws. It was a whole lot of nonsense anyway, to a cat. She had four feet to look out for and she never tripped over them. In fact, no matter what happened, she was likely to land on them squarely and walk away. It wasn't difficult. People made things far too complicated.

'I couldn't agree more, Socrates, you wise old thing. We muddle things up because we need to know everything, thus confusing it all and mudding the waters.' She rested in her straight backed chair, and swivelled it round to look out yet another window.

This window looked indirectly into the backyard, where the angophora gum she regularly spoke with these days, stood.

Socrates leaped up on the window sill and she found herself absently patting the cat, as they both looked into the past. It was more than okay to pat a cat when it asked for it. Socrates was never backward in coming forward about what she wanted.

She watched from her window the gradual flow of the day. When she was younger, the days had stretched out with seeming endless hours to be filled. Then came the time when they had settled back into the ebb and flow; the rhythm of the Universe. The days were exactly the speed she wanted them to be. Now, just when she needed the days to stay steady, she could feel them running away from her: fleeing in front of her, as though time itself was determined to hasten away.

And she didn't have any to waste. She'd promised herself long ago that ninety was the age she would die, and ninety it was going to be. She'd thought she had nothing more to do, so ninety would work well. But lately she had important things to do and with time flittering through her fingers, she felt she'd lost the ability to control it. She allowed herself to get trapped in the dream and lost her own reality.

It was very frustrating.

The world she looked out at had shrunk: to the garden, the neighbourhood, a few shops and Socrates. The few visitors who did still come made little or no dent in the increasing solitude of her life.

'The smaller the world out there becomes, Socrates, the larger my world in here grows,' she told the cat, who was well aware of this fact, living as she did, in every Moment of the Now in a way her human was only just beginning to understand.

'Not only are we all walking backwards, trying to discover the answers to a question we haven't even asked yet, but we are searching in far flung places for pieces of ourselves we never lost. Or at least, we didn't lose them in places we've never been.'

Socrates gave up. These were lessons she'd tried to impart for more than ten years and it bored her to listen to them again. With one last glance at the view, Socrates curled up, folding her tail securely over her nose and promptly fell asleep.

She glanced at the cat and smiled. The uncomplicated way Socrates viewed things was harder for a person to achieve.

What had been a random conversation with a tree so long ago had become a full blown experience of opening her mind to the potential that all human life forms could communicate with anything and everything that they wished to. They just had to learn how and have the patience to keep practicing. No one learned to speak a second language overnight and yet every day, people all over the world sat down and meditated for five minutes for five days and wondered why they hadn't had a vision. Or the Heavens hadn't opened up and spoken forth on the answer to their questions.

There was more to learning to speak to the Divine than closing one's eyes one day and crossing fingers on the left or right hand, depending on the personal superstition. Crossing one's eyes, toes or legs, wasn't going to help either.

PART II: IN THE BEGINNING

Hard work – no laughing matter

It had come as a nasty shock one day at the end of university, when final marks were presented and degrees awarded (or not), to realise that one's days of learning were to come to an end and one was expected to become an adult; whatever that meant.

It was even more of a shock to realise that the wild dreams of youth, dreamt while lying under the shade of leafy trees, on bright green grass with the whole world laid out before her, were to be packed away and forgotten. Princesses didn't get to kiss toads, who became princes (just toads who stayed unhelpfully toads). The only thing that happened when you let down your hair was a hangover the next day and the horrid thought that you couldn't remember the name of the boy next to you. You didn't get to climb down from your prison and escape to a magical world with yet another prince (there seemed to be an extraordinary amount of princes to go around in the books and yet so very few in real life).

And the worst thing to realise, after all this time of daydreaming and believing in the extraordinary, was that:

'I'm ordinary,' she lamented.

Most of her friends were pretty ordinary, as well. They didn't seem to worry.

But she did.

It was immensely frustrating to flick through a magazine full of not ordinary people, and look up and watch the not ordinary glamorous girls around them. Her friends didn't complain. They'd found ordinary to be okay: sufficient, if nothing better.

But she was used to dreaming of things she couldn't quite remember; but she knew in those dreams nothing had been ordinary, especially not her.

While in the throes of youthful exuberance, she had planned things to do with her life. And sitting around waiting for someone to come along and rescue her wasn't her style. If there was rescuing to be done, she rationalised, she would be the one who did it, regardless of the stories of princes. Everything was possible in the minds of youth.

This all had flashed through her childlike mind in one blinding instant lighting up her internal world like neon. The only trouble was time; and a constant deluge of rules and advice that spoke of ordinariness and waiting. That happiness was not to be pursued and women didn't rescue themselves.

Someone did it for them, didn't you know? It said so in all the movies and TV shows and romance novels. Her father said so, and if he said it, it must be so.

As time crept along, she lost interest in the theme. The idea of rescuing anything, let alone herself, slowly faded. Her parents worked and came home tired and irritable. They told her to work hard at school and she just might be able to make something of herself: though they were in a little bit of doubt about this because, well, if truth had to be told, she was an odd child.

She liked to be alone. She liked to talk to the fairies that lived, according to her, in the circle of rocks she'd created under the mulberry tree. When in season, they could find her clinging precariously to branches, throwing mulberries down to the fairies: one for her, one for them.

Her parents thought it was disturbing that she continued to do this well into high school.

They hoped that this tendency to stay with the fey and inhabit worlds that didn't exist would slowly fade. So they drummed into her head that time wasn't on her side. She'd grow up soon and need to stand on her own two feet. They weren't getting any younger, and wanted her to have a good job to settle down into before they popped their clogs.

Their words: not hers.

But she clung to the ridiculous notion that dreams were inspiring and could be real, and that work was only work because people hated it.

Until one day, she didn't.

That day, she graduated and her father passed away soon after she started university.

It was then that she realised nothing was going to be the same ever again. And that he had been right all along. Dreams were stupid toys little girls dressed up like dolls, to play with in the early morning of their lives, only to be tossed aside come the reality of midday.

The idea of growing old with her folks always there to explain things to her and help her make decisions, went out the window. She was cast adrift. If she had still been dreaming, she would have described herself as floating in an ocean, with no map and no boat, just lying on her back trying to navigate with the stars. Only she'd never read them before.

She'd taken a job and accepted her place in university. Her father had always insisted that there was nothing in this world like a top rate education.

'You mark my words, young lady. Boys will come and go. So let them. But your mind is your greatest asset and don't you let anyone ever tell you different. Once you have educated yourself, a solid job will see you through. *Then* you can allow yourself to be distracted by boys. It'll be the right time to find a partner and raise a family. Don't try to do that without a proper job. You'll get too far into debt.'

Those words rang in her ears for many years to come. She never quite managed to silence him. Not until she started listening to something else.

And she didn't suppose back then she would find more in common with a tree.

'What was it you always wanted to be?' a friend asked her once.

No one had asked her that for quite some time. University days were done. They'd all graduated and gone out to get better jobs. Or so they thought. That was what was done after you managed to get qualified. No matter how you felt about it on the inside.

She no longer found working behind the counter the sort of thing someone as educated as she was, was expected to do. With education, she realised, came all sorts of expectations. Her father hadn't warned her about that. She guessed he had believed she would only worry about *his* expectations and the rest could be damned.

All the people she had met and the fun she had had behind her little counter. Now, she was educated. There was no time in her life to have that sort of fun. She was meant to be at work.

You never had fun at work.

So she left retail and the fun of meeting new people and talking to them about their lives and the interesting things they did. She left the satisfaction of finding them exactly what they wanted or needed, and the smiles they gave her in gratitude. One customer even bought her a rose just because she was overtired and her feet were sore that day.

She was ever so grateful. It had been a lovely gesture.

It just wasn't done, though.

She now had the university education her father wanted her to have and her mother needed looking after. So she left the job where there were smiles and laughter and people appreciated her singing as she packed the shelves, waltzing down the aisles.

And she found an office job.

Now this was work, real honest to goodness work. She knew her father would be proud of her, wherever he was. She wasn't one to think about that sort of thing. People just died, didn't they? There wasn't anything but complete blackness, and a cessation of the worry that came with being alive.

She clung to this idea, even though she contradictorily thought of him as watching over her and nodding in approval as she worked.

Because working was boring and mundane and repetitive, and no one there laughed. If they did, it was in the coffee room or behind their hands, as though it was a crime. A bit like coughing when you have the flu: covering your mouth because you might spread the infection.

Laughter wasn't frowned upon, management told their slaves - it was merely a distraction. Everyone wanted to know what the laughter was about. This led to discussion. This led to people stopping what they were meant to be doing. Work would pause. Reports wouldn't get written and files wouldn't get... filed. This was NOT ON.

So laughter ceased.

She wondered if it was possible to forget how to laugh at all? Was it like riding a bicycle? Even if she didn't do it for years, she could just hop back on and all would be well?

Or was it more like driving a manual car? Years down the track, after being in an automatic, you were confronted with a stick shift and clutch: instant panic. You had no idea of what to do next.

She wondered if this was the case for all office work. Surely, she decided, not everyone thought that offices were cages and buildings were prisons? There had to be a place out there where she could make her father proud and still laugh.

It just might be possible, she had to concede, that because she was ordinary she was doomed to repeat those reports forever.

How she hated being ordinary.

Mousey brown hair, with mousey brown eyes, average height, average weight, average clothing sense: everything about her was ordinary and average.

Not for her were the bright colours of spring, or the pastels of autumn. She was okay with her ordinary wardrobe. Neat trouser suits with white blouses. It paid to stay in the bounds of a uniform.

You never got lost with a uniform. You knew what suited you and what suited the job, and there you were – all set up for life.

Her father had had two suits.

One for work. One for funerals. The one for funerals doubled as one for weddings.

He'd had four ties. One was 'just in case'. She never did find out in case of what. The only thing her father hadn't stinted on was shirts.

'You can't have too many shirts. They say a lot about the man. Strong colours and plain. You only have stripes in your shirts on the weekend. And you have to make sure that the stripes match the ties you have.'

He was very good at dispensing advice.

Not so hot on taking it.

So she had two suits. Two plain trouser suits because skirts weren't something she had ever felt comfortable in. Her mother had grown up in skirts. They were like the straight jacket of a generation.

But as the skirt hem had gone up, her desire to wear one went down. Her mother had told her that short skirts were improper, and for someone with thicker ankles, it wasn't the done thing to show them. She had to agree. She did have thicker ankles. Showing them would somehow seem rude, so she wore long trouser suits and tailored shirts.

One black suit and one navy. White shirts or black shirts went with them. On weekends, there were tracksuit pants and T-shirts, all of muted colours. Not for her the rainbow of choice. That would lead her to think that perhaps the ankles weren't that bad and how about that nice pair of shorts and tank top?

No, her father had ideas about tank tops on women. He had ideas of tank tops on men, too.

'Muscle bound buffoons. Idiots, the lot of them. Waltzing around, pretending that what they look like counts. Well it does. But it doesn't say anything good about them, let me tell you.'

He ended up telling her a lot.

'If they had exercised the muscle between their ears half as much as the muscle on their arms, they'd be wearing a suit and earning themselves some serious money. Don't think you'll be dating one of those, young lady. We won't have that type of person in our family.'

She diplomatically didn't mention cousin Devon, who regularly went to a gym, dated a model and wore as little as he could. Devon was hardly mentioned at all, unless he was held up as a 'case in point'.

When her father decided she needed an example of 'what not to be', Devon and his model of a girlfriend (depending on which one it was that week) were always used as a 'case in point'. She kept to herself the wistfulness she felt when she thought of Devon and his freedom to do and be whatever he wanted to be even if it didn't match up to what her father thought was proper. And as for his girlfriend! She thought it would be nice to have slender ankles.

She bought a running suit once.

Just the once. It was taken to the skip bin for the needy. Her mother had been so horrified to see her in it, she'd almost had palpitations. There was no need for that sort of thing in this house, thank you very much.

'We eat well and watch our weight. No need for a young woman to wear something so revolting and revealing. There is no need to get all worked up and sweaty. We'd never let you get fat, dear,' said her mother.

And indeed they didn't. The only parts of her that wasn't average were those thick ankles.

She turned sideways and looked at herself in the mirror. The whole image reeked of ordinary. From the plain shoes with laces tied neatly, to the hair neatly combed into place.

Shoes were a passion, but not a passion she had spent a lot of time cultivating. Shoes were supposed to be a tool. They helped keep your feet clean and dry and your posture straight, according to her mother. Nothing said bad posture more than heels higher than two centimetres. Nothing was more useless than open toed shoes, as who had time to paint toenails or to make sure the hair on the big toe wasn't showing?

No, the only thing to do was to buy plain laced shoes or court shoes for summer. They went with everything. Nothing worse than opening up your wardrobe and not being able to decide what to wear just because you didn't have the right pair of shoes, is there?

'Don't let vanity rule your life, dear. Have a white pair, a black pair and a navy pair of shoes. They are always in fashion, they'll protect your feet and you won't grow up with bunions. Look at Aunt Clara's feet. My sister wore the most outrageous heels when she was younger. Did she listen to me? No, she did not. And now look at her. She can hardly walk with those feet of hers.'

There was no telling her mother that Aunt Clara's feet had never recovered from a botched operation to rid her of arthritis. As far as her mother was concerned, the only thing responsible for 'those feet', as she called them, was Aunt Clara's passion for heels.

'Any size! One inch, three inches high. The woman was insatiable. She had to have a pair in every colour, in every sized heel and many of them were *strappy*.'

Said with overtones of such acute horror she almost expected Aunt Clara to break out in devil's horns the next time they went to visit.

So no, she didn't indulge her passion for shoes. She wished she had the courage to take home a pair of red high heels.

Though mother would probably pop her clogs on the spot.

Today was the day. She was going to laugh in the office and apply online to the job offered down the road. Surely there was a place for her. A workplace where she could fill her father's impossibly large shoes, work hard, get a mortgage and find a husband? Where she could use her impressive degree and laugh at the same time. The joy wasn't going to vanish out of her life.

She glanced one more time in the mirror.

Well, not completely anyway. There were faint traces of joy around her mouth and edging her eyes. They would not be wiped clean. For all her mother made her wear a hat so she didn't squint, and wrinkle cream, though she was still in her twenties.

'You can't be too blasé about the fight for wrinkle-free skin. They'll catch you unawares and one day you'll have a face like a road map. Until you get a husband you have to make sure that age doesn't show, my dear. Men don't like road maps.'

She didn't say, 'Men don't mind maps, Mother. It's asking for directions that they are lousy at.' She wasn't too sure her mother would get the humour. There was still the possibility she'd get her mouth washed out with soap.

But she couldn't allow that to sway her now. It was onwards and upwards this day. The new job was in a better department, though still working for the government. But this new department had a higher ratio of men to women. If she couldn't find someone to complete the picture of wedded bliss there, then she was stumped.

Perhaps there was something wrong with her?

She shook her head.

There wasn't. She was perfectly ordinary: nothing wrong with that.

She had already forgotten how hard she had fought to be anything but ordinary. The idea that ordinary wasn't for her and that she could be something more had died along with the green grass she had dreamt upon, and the soft spring of youth.

Ordinary would just have to do. There was plenty of time to find the husband, be completed and feel like a contributing part of the human race.

She tugged the jacket into place and headed to work.

She scurried along, her face just as grim as all the others. She could feel it in the tightness of her jaw, the thinness of her lips and the tension between her shoulders. She glanced sideways at those who walked with her.

Did she really look like that?

Head down, eyes narrowed, blankly thinking of what report needed to be written. There were old joy lines on many of these faces. But they had forgotten to allow it to show. The lines were fading and overlaid with thick heavier lines of wear and tear.

She wondered why it was called the human race. Though, when she looked down from her office and saw the others scurrying from place to place, it was all too easy to see.

They raced: to be first, to have the most, to be the best, to hoard more. Scrambling, they clawed their way to the top, only to stand there and look at the next mountain and begin again. She wondered if they ever took the time to enjoy the view.

Slipping into her seat, she started the computer. There was still time to change her mind. She hadn't sent the application yet. She'd stayed back last night, and filled in all the forms and saved them on her hard drive. Her mother thought it was a wonderful sign of impending promotion that she was home late. She didn't have the heart to say it wasn't hard work that kept her, only an application. If she got it, there would a small pay rise. Perhaps that would smooth things over at home when she explained she'd moved jobs.

'Tenacity, that's the key. You get a good job and you stick to it. Why would a company bother to train you and promote you if they thought you were going to leave? Give them no cause to doubt your loyalty. Stay with them. Job security isn't a dirty word,' said her father.

There was no explaining to him now. Governments were large, faceless and uncaring employers. People came and went all the time. The government didn't care.

There was no CEO, no bottom line. There were just reports, and files, endless files. She didn't think anyone would notice if she went. There would still be reports to do. She had no doubt there would be reports to do in the next department, as well. They would just take her file and change her number, and then she'd be seated behind another computer. She wondered when it had become okay that thousands of people were just numbers. Millions, if you counted every person who worked for any sort of government.

They were all servants of the public: though none appeared to be serving anything.

She had the feeling that the government was a living breathing organism that ate people up. Thirty years later it spat out a corpse and allowed it to walk around until it fell over, all life and joy and laughter drained right out. It was as if the stuffing was left behind.

Underneath her acceptance of work, she had a feeling. Something wasn't right. The stuffing was meant to stay on the inside. But people just patched themselves up and kept going back to work. She saw little grey people with jackets that had leather patches on the elbows. She wondered if it was possible to put a patch where her soul was leaking out.

She wondered if there was such a thing as a soul in the first place.

Because if there was, then these soulless jobs were bound to suck it right out of her. The machine would roll right along while she sank below the surface, patches on her elbows.

But that wasn't the next step. The next step was to get another job.

'There are jobs out there that people enjoy, you know,' a colleague told her. 'About one third of jobs in the government actually mean something. They are the ones people die in. They don't move out of them and you can only grab one when the last person goes out, boots and all.'

She could totally understand that. People even passed up promotions to keep the good jobs. There had to be a sense of job satisfaction somewhere and she was on a mission to find it. There was nothing in the rule book of life her father had drummed into her that said some level of satisfaction could not be found in work. Hard work didn't equal lack of joy. Not for everyone, and there was something flickering in the depths of her mind that wanted to believe she would be one of those people. There was a job out there for her with some laughter still attached.

So her mission was to find that joy.

There was the not so quiet voice of her father in her head when she hit the send button - 'It's good that you are aiming higher. Sitting around doing a job you are too qualified for won't help matters. You don't want to appear too ambitious, or the young men will think you believe you're smarter than them. But you don't want to appear to enjoy slacking off at the bottom of the heap. No man will seriously attach himself to someone who doesn't strive.'

She wasn't too sure what the happy medium was. Striking the balance between appearing too brilliant and not outshining anyone wasn't for the faint hearted. She knew she had a brain. The whole idea, she once believed, with getting a good education was to prove once and for all, she was smart. But of course, it wasn't that easy.

'Not too smart' were watch words to look out for. Bosses felt threatened if you produced too much work in too short a time frame. Seeing as they were mainly men, she decided early on not to work *too* hard or appear too smart. There was a balance in that, as well.

The trouble was, she was soon to realise, this rule applied to women as well. The few times she'd had a female boss and tried to show she could excel, she'd been railroaded. Women, she realised, didn't want you to be good at anything – even worse to some extent than a man. They prided themselves on being the only woman in the office who was efficient and if you stepped on their toes – look out.

Those she'd met in some of her workplaces couldn't be trusted. This was a theme with her father too. People in general couldn't be trusted, and no one would look out for you, and you had to do it all yourself (until you got a husband and he did it for you). She wondered if women really were designed to tear strips off each other. Instead of working together, they bitched about what she was wearing, or who was seeing whom. The two female bosses she'd had, knowing she was smarter than they were, kept her out of the loop. They didn't forward her emails; gave her half the information she needed to get the job done so she looked like a fool to the others. They kept her bored and useless, and complained to upper management she wasn't pulling her weight.

So she started to apply the 'not too smart' rule in all things, at home and at work.

It was little wonder she felt as though she was walking a tightrope through life. There were so many rules. She was surprised at how many people still managed to find time to do outrageous things like throwing themselves out of planes, or off cliffs. There was a small part inside that wondered if her father's rule book, unwritten but much thumbed through, was just a little too detailed. But when she thought things like that, she could hear him saying:

'People don't understand what it takes to have a harmonious society these days. The wild behaviour of young people shows a lack of steady character. You don't want to prove you have a lack of steadiness about you. That's a dead turn off, in the workplace and in the home. Steady as she goes, young lady. This frivolity is unseemly. I'm glad you don't seem to be infected with it.'

Sometimes she wondered if it was possible to get the infection. It seemed so glamorous to be off partying on a weekday, with work the next day. At lunchtime, those who had this infection would fly out of the office, letting loose all the laughter they had consumed while writing reports. They would roll along on the joy of having frivolity infecting their lives. She would look longingly at them and wish they'd breathe on her. Perhaps her ordinariness would melt like snow and she too would become daring and fascinating, with curling lips painted in colour and laughter trailing behind her.

It wasn't as though she didn't laugh. Oh no, there was a time and a place for all things. In her own quiet way, she was quite popular. People found she would listen to anything. This was always in demand, because people loved to talk about themselves.

They weren't so quick to listen.

Because she wasn't involved in a life of frivolity, she would concentrate on every word that came out of their mouths, as though it was gold.

'You're amazing,' one friend told her, giving her a hug. 'I always feel as though I am the centre of your life when I talk to you. You do *have* other friends, don't you?'

This was asked with a slight frown of worry. No one wanted to be friends with a crazy woman. She would laugh and nod, and move to the next person. It wasn't that she didn't have other friends. But people's lives were so full, they lived as though they were throwing themselves forward and she knew she was caged with all the rules in her life.

They were so free. Free in their heartbreaks, their loves and losses. They were so free with vital information about themselves. They threw their lives, their entire entities around like confetti, spraying the world with words about themselves. It was scary to her how far people would go with the retelling of their lives to her.

But it was endlessly fascinating.

They were just so fascinating she couldn't think of anything else when they were telling her about themselves. Even the ones who were more like her. She realised it was life *itself* that was fascinating. What each person did with it in their own unique way. People like her, who followed the rules laid down by generations of hard workers, and people who *weren't* ordinary like she was, who partied and laughed and waved their hands about with glittering rings on fingers tipped with red. No matter how many she met and talked to, there wasn't one story out of their mouths that was the same.

The endless variety was breathtaking and dizzying. Her father certainly hadn't warned her about that.

22

Love – and other untrustworthy people

'You'll meet a lot of people over the years,' he said, puffing on his pipe. A filthy habit, her mother called it. But one you put up with when the man in your life was such a good provider.

'They'll come in all sorts of guises, but remember one thing. Unless it's your husband, then they aren't ever really trustworthy.'

Mother smiled at him. It was okay to indulge the man of the house, she was told. If he wanted to talk to you about such stuff, you were expected to pay some attention. And if he wanted to befoul the house with pipe smoke, well, could you really say no? He was paying for the house, after all. You had to stop working when the children came. There was no time to prepare dinner, wash clothes, vacuum houses and press his shirts if you kept working. So if he wanted to smoke in the house (and give you all lung cancer), then it was his right.

She didn't think that her mother was right about that. But her father had nodded his head sagely and told her that men had the need to unwind after a hard day's work, and seeing as the wife didn't do all that much, was it too much to ask that she indulge this one thing?

'People will try to rob you blind. There are con artists on every street corner and 'added extras' in just about every contract. So don't you go signing anything unless your husband has read it first. They'll trick a woman out of her last penny. Your mother bought a course, once. I didn't mind, mind you, it does a woman good to keep improving herself. I don't believe that nonsense about women not being educated, so you make sure you get a good education, you hear?'

Most conversations could be brought around to the idea of education. It fascinated him. He thought he'd done his best to keep her mother educated, even though they had married young and the children came soon after. The fact that there were so many miscarriages

23

and only one offspring wasn't anyone's fault, he'd magnanimously explained.

'Anyway, she bought this course and hadn't read the fine print.' He looked at her mother with fond exasperation. 'There were so many books and subject choices, and all of them at extra cost; you didn't get the qualification unless you'd done so many of the subjects. Your choice as to which ones, but they all cost a bundle. Crooks, I told them. Preying on the mother of a house while her husband is at work, it just isn't done.'

But there were all sorts of people who would take advantage if they could. A young woman all by herself in the world was just the sort of target they enjoyed.

Don't go out alone, because there were rapists everywhere. Groups were the only way to avoid them. They could sniff out a vulnerable girl from the other side of town, apparently. No dates alone with young men until you learned a bit more about the world, but it was hard to do that when you weren't allowed out alone. But that sort of inconsistency wasn't pointed out, because then you were sent to your room.

No one could take advantage of you if there was a proper mix of young men and young women in one group (No one could get to know someone special privately, either).

Eventually, there was the maiden voyage of one-on-one dating. This came after a lecture on manners.

'If he doesn't open your car door, the door of the restaurant and hold out your chair, then you know you have a problem. He might not be the kind of young man who will take no for an answer, so you get a waiter to phone me. I'll come and get you.

'If his palms are sweaty when he tries to hold your hand, because believe me they all take that sort of liberty one time or another, then he's got filthy things on his mind. You phone home as soon as you can and I'll come and get you.

'If he makes any lurid jokes, innuendos or implies that you are the kind of girl who would go home with him, then you phone me. That sort of thing will not be tolerated. And if you aren't home by eleven, I'm phoning the police.'

These things went round and round in her mind on that first date. The young man was as nervous as she was. He didn't try to hold her hand, but she saw him wiping them down his trouser leg a few times.

She didn't mention this to her father when she got home. Mainly because she'd wiped hers down her skirt in the preparation of holding the hand that was never offered. She didn't want to have to admit to that and be forced to explain her thoughts at the time.

Mainly, she'd been trying to work out if the boy had 'ideas' and if so, was she prepared to allow him to follow through? There was the horrid thought in the back of her mind that she might never get the opportunity to go out like this again, because her fear of what *might* happen could outweigh any remembered pleasure. If that happened, she wanted the remembered pleasure to be bloody *impressive*. Plus, one friend had told her all about snogging this chap over the last weekend and it sounded just the thing to experiment with. Not too advanced (for the beginner more advanced moves should be avoided at all cost) but pleasant, all the same.

But the more she stared at the chap opposite her, weighing all this up in her mind, the further away the possibility became. For some reason, the more she looked, the more times he wiped his hands down his trouser legs. Nerves were one thing, but he must have had some very lurid thoughts to require that much wiping off.

She'd gone home, ungroped, unkissed, with her hands still pristine, though slightly damp. He hadn't rung again.

That brought her to the realisation that there was a lot of truth in what her mother and father told her.

'They'll break your heart, dear,' said her mother. 'Until I met your father, I thought all men were – well, best not to mention that. They won't phone when they promise to, they try to touch you most inappropriately and they'll leave you the minute they've had their way.'

It was true, she realised soon after that first date. She'd meet men who would smile at her and twinkle with their eyes. They had the same idea and would never phone after they went home alone. She wondered why her male friends, a select few who didn't seem to care if she didn't sleep with them, were insulted by the way women viewed their sex.

'It's not fair. They're all such bitter bitches. It's not like *I've* ever hurt her,' complained one, when his date dumped her wine over his head.

Upon further probing, he admitted he'd asked her back to his place. It was their first date.

'I'd had a bit too much to drink and my place was walking distance.

I wasn't driving her home with a tank full. I'd be pulled up for sure. Anyway, I was horny.'

That, when it boiled down to it, seemed to be the defence of all her mates. She tried to explain that a lifetime of men only wanting to have a few beers and get into their pants had turned women off for life, but they weren't listening. What would she know, they asked? She wasn't lowering that draw bridge for anyone.

They had a point, she conceded. But the heartbroken tears of friends who had slept with the man of their dreams, only to discover he was really the devil in disguise, had left a sour taste in her mouth. That and her father's warning.

'You'll never find a truly decent husband if you've been around the block a few times. It's not appealing in any way. Decent men want a decent woman. The ones who go around the block with you will always leave. You get that ring on your finger first. They'll take advantage if they can.'

She lived in constant fear that her heart would be ripped out by a man who smiled at her and promised her the moon, then left her in the dirt once he'd had his way. She was afraid her own judgement on that sort of thing wasn't all that great. But she did know that if the man was devastatingly gorgeous, he wasn't interested in spending time with her for anything but one thing. Ordinary women like her didn't end up with extraordinary men like them.

When her father died, a part of her died too. The part that needed support and guidance freaked out. But she held onto the lessons in her head. That was the one good thing about him always repeating them. They stuck.

Eventually, however, like all young ladies, she decided that a taste of the forbidden fruit wouldn't go astray. She had cultivated logic and a practical sense of self for a while before this happened. She believed anything was possible if she put her mind to it, even choosing the right man for this Great Experiment.

She went out with her girlfriends and studied the playing field. There were many lovely men out there; it was the final moments of university after all. But she needed one that wasn't going to be around for very long, just in case she was stupid, like she often suspected she might be, and fell in love with him. So she picked a foreigner and had a drink.

One drink led to more than one, and finally he took her hand and led her outside.

Kissing, she discovered, was a *highly* addictive sport. Her father prattled along in the back of her head, advising her against this irregular course of action, but she managed to squish him for once.

While she would have been quite content to kiss for hours and never move, that wasn't the agenda. The young man had different ideas. For which, in a way, she was grateful because she was sure she wouldn't have been able to find the courage to make the next step herself. She wasn't even sure what the next step was. In concept, yes: in practice, the idea of making the next move didn't seem very feasible.

Luckily, he had definite plans and moved things along quite nicely.

It wasn't his fault she'd never done this before and the whole experiment went sadly flat. She suddenly realised why some of her girlfriends were swearing off boys for life and going out with girls. She wondered if *that* was the next step.

If all men were just like her mother warned, and all people were just like her father warned, then she really did need to look out for herself. Experimenting with life seemed to be the only way forward. That way, she could stay safely removed from the outcome. Scientists never appeared to be moved by their own experiments.

Finding someone new and feminine with which to experiment with, however, was not as easy as with a boy.

Boys were all out for the same thing. They got tarted up, bench pressed a bit to swell their muscles so they looked good in the shirt they'd picked out; stuffed a handful of condoms in wallets (they were always optimistically hopeful about their own prowess); and went out to get pissed. Along the way, if they found a likely enough target who gave them the nod, it was all systems go. There was always some chap up for it. So to speak. Mainly because there were always more boys ready to jump into the sack, she realised, than there were women. Girls liked to go out to enjoy themselves. Boys were not always on their radar.

Girls were a harder quarry to hunt down.

They sat in groups, enjoyed each other's company, smiled nicely when a bloke offered them a drink (sometimes took it too, knowing full well they weren't going to go home with the sucker, but well, who knocked back a free drink?) and danced together.

However, they did not wear some sort of 'tag' that said 'am open to the approach of another woman.'

27

This was going to cause issues, she could tell. She couldn't just go around asking. And she couldn't ask her friends the best way to go about this. She loved her friends. She really did. And she enjoyed them talking to her about everything under the sun. She felt very lucky that they trusted her like that.

But she didn't. Trust like that. Cold shivers crawled down her back even thinking about talking to anyone about her new experiment, because they'd be bound to tell someone. You couldn't trust people not to gossip. One way or another, everyone would find out and her mother would be horrified. More than horrified. Disgusted!

Plus, it was an experiment. Everyone would be horrified. Her girl friends were still talking about things like love and relationships. They cried big fat droplets of heartache when things didn't work out. They didn't think that the next time it might be the same old thing. They tried again (and again and again) each time with the hope in their eyes that he might stay. That he might be the one to bandage the wounds, cover over the scars, and make things all right in their world.

They hoped that they could hand over the fragile crystal ball that was their heart and he'd treasure it, holding it so lightly in his hands as not to break it, but so firmly it would never fall.

Each time they cried.

So she had to plan the whole thing on her own.

The girls who had sworn off boys were suddenly her best friends. She went to all their parties, their bars and listened to all their gossip. In the gossip were some very helpful tips on the right way to go about this thing called love. Though she was determined it wasn't going to be. Love. She had a pathological fear of that term.

Boundaries, babies, husbands who smoked inside, and wouldn't let her pay the bills.

No, university wasn't for love. It was for experimenting.

Love would come later, when she had the job that was 'hard work' and the money to show she was a good, moderately ambitious earner who would be content to let her man take care of her when she had a baby. She rather thought that was a lot to ask of one little job, but her father should know. She watched her friends claw their way through the morass out there and wondered why they all looked for love in the places where all they found where jackasses.

Surely, she thought, you'd start to look somewhere else.

If boys were all hot, heavy, and so fast and energetic she felt jack hammered into place (where did they get the idea that that was fun?), girls were the opposite. She was quite sure that there would be girls out there who were equal to the task, like a man. But she was looking for opposites and she got them.

Soft lips, slow and gentle touch. Lots of touch. No moving from touch until begged, even then, maybe not. Discovering her breasts were not mounds of dough to be pummelled into place; nor the actual act a desperate race to see who could finish first. No two guesses as to who that had been when she was with her boy.

The evening was romantic, special and she woke up feeling completely different.

But something was missing, so she didn't go back. Plus, it had been harder to find a woman of the necessary persuasion who wasn't staying around. She didn't want them to be there in the morning. Well, perhaps the morning, but not the following day, or next week. What part of – this isn't love - didn't they get?

She didn't trust that the little adventure would stay just between the two of them, so she made sure it wasn't going to happen again. Sad really, considering. There was no stubble rash to worry about.

But that ended the experimenting stage. She realised that things never worked out as you hoped. She went out looking for the science and got ones who wanted to follow her home. Her friends went out looking for love and found an endless stream of love rats. She couldn't allow that to happen to her. She couldn't trust that it wouldn't, so best not to go there. Wait till everyone grew up a bit. Then perhaps she might trust someone enough to open her heart.

The seals were rusting away. She just didn't know it yet.

Love has a funny way of sneaking up on you when you least expect it. While she was studying hard, preparing to go out into the work force and find the other half of her rather ordinary existence, she found love in the usual way.

'You must keep your head down while you're studying, dear. There are so many distractions. Girls are their own worst enemies. Just when freedom and a good steady job are around the corner, they become distracted. So many girls in my class didn't even finish their leaving certificate. They fell in love, lost the will to study, and went and got married instead. Don't let that happen to you.' Her mother's words rang in her head.

So when her friends finally found 'the one' and started getting engaged at the end of their final year at university, she turned her face from love. It was a distraction. It broke your heart; boys would promise you the moon and never deliver.

Her mother was sure that the only way to find a lasting relationship was to get that hard working job and prove that you were a woman of some substance. A man would want a partner who could prove herself.

'I found your father in the office, dear. I had just moved from the typing pool into the main office and he was at the desk next to the boss's office. He was going places, I could tell. It made all the others just pea green with envy when he would stop past my desk and chat. To me! When we started walking out on dates, I just knew this would be the one. He didn't try any of that funny business and was always where he said he would be, including on the end of the phone calling me when he promised. A real keeper.'

She knew all she had to do was hold on, get past all the distractions of university (and stop her experimenting) and she would be fine. A good job, a good man, and happiness would follow. That was how it was meant to be. She tried not to think of the lines of bitterness that her mother insisted were age lines, framing her mother's mouth.

Was she really happy? Had her father showed up and given her mother the happiness she deserved? Was he truly the other half of her life?

She pondered on these questions, when she watched the boys walking past. Was there anyone out there who could help her be less ordinary, because she wasn't so much worried about the happiness angle. Her mother had assured her that it wasn't what people thought. It came and went, dipping into your life one moment and hiding the next.

'You'll be lucky if the happiest moments of your life keep you warm at night, dear. If you can always remember them and hold them close, like a treasure, you'll be fine.'

So happiness was elusive. But to her it was the idea of being ordinary; rearing its ugly head once more now university was drawing to a close.

'I can't go through my whole life being ordinary,' she explained to a close friend, one day at lunch. 'I sometimes feel as though life is choking me. Do you get that feeling?'

The other girl laughed at her.

'You come out with the strangest things. I think that's why we're friends. I never know what you're thinking or about to say. Being ordinary is a gift. It would be horrid to be stupid, or even worse, someone of interest. Could you imagine what it must be like to have people follow you around, or have photos taken while you were swimming? Or everyone commenting on your fat, or bones or whatever? No thanks. I like to blend.'

She wondered about that. Did she like to blend? There was a lot going for blending. People didn't worry about what you were up to every day. You could eat a pie with chips and a beer, and the world didn't draw a disgusted breath on how bad your diet was.

On the other hand, she thought, it might be nice to be noticed. To have someone pay attention to everything you did and said and thought. For once. She loved her parents, but they handed out advice, she had come to realise, without actually ever stopping to ask her how her day had been.

With thoughts like these in her head, it was little wonder that love struck a blow when she least expected it.

'How long have we been friends?' he asked, munching on a sandwich.

She watched as some mayonnaise trickled out the side, sneakily, so he couldn't see it. It was amazing how fascinating he could make eating a lettuce, tomato and mayonnaise sandwich. She knew he'd catch that pesky little white blob. He always did. He always had the same sandwich and every day, a part of it tried to escape, and every day he caught it just before it managed to.

Sure enough, he tilted the sandwich to the side and flicked out his tongue. It darted between his fingers and up the side of his sandwich, taking all the mayonnaise with it. None escaped. She smiled. He had such a marvellous way of dealing with the small details of eating. He also had strong looking fingers, she realised. That was something she had never really thought about before. She frowned. Somewhere in the back of her head warning bells were ringing.

A part of her brain remembered a friend telling her that attention to small details was a sure sign of something more than friendship.

She squished the thought flat and took her eyes off his fingers.

'Ages. Beyond ages. We were friends even before we met,' she joked, trying to cover the awkwardness in her mind.

They'd met at school. He'd been a late transfer for the last two years at her high school and they'd pretty much been inseparable since. Her father didn't object because she had promised her mother she wasn't being distracted, that in fact he helped her with her school work, and he was going out with one of the ballerinas. When they met, her father looked at her friend and saw a younger version of himself. His words.

She didn't see that. She saw a friend who could break down calculus so she could understand it. Someone who helped her see the magic in Shakespeare even though his words were archaic and all his books needed to be burned. Her words.

Now, she could see other things.

She saw a man who ate sandwiches with strong square teeth, who had long fingers that had little tuffs of black hair on their knuckles. A man who was about to finish a degree in pure math and possibly go on to do honours. Who had doubled this degree with English because the magic of poetry and the English language shouldn't stop at the end of high school. His words.

They were close. But she had never told him about her experiments. There was a part of her that was too ashamed. She had gone out there and *picked up*. It was her mother's worst nightmare. And her father wouldn't have spoken to her again, she was more than sure.

This was her high school mate who had shared everything with her, including their last pimples. She'd felt from the start they had known each other all the days of their lives.

It just seemed that lately, he'd changed. Or she'd changed. Anyway, something had changed and he was looking very... nice. Handsome, even, definitely smart - always had been.

He glanced over at her and their eyes met.

An everyday occurrence, she tried to remind herself. But for some reason, the thoughts in her head wouldn't stay put and colour crept up her cheeks. If he asks me a question now, she thought, I won't have an answer. I can't think of a single thing.

But he didn't. He didn't ask her anything for quite a few minutes, not in words. There are a lot of different ways to ask someone the sorts of questions that were flying around in his mind.

Kissing someone for five minutes worked very well, for starters.

She had never been an 'item' before. It felt strange, similar to being friends with someone, but far far more intense. Everything became more intense.

The world took on such a glow, she felt like she was seeing it all for the first time. Why, oh why, did her friends think things were difficult? This was Love and this was wonderful. They didn't understand. It wasn't going to end and they didn't need to worry. He was everything her parents had ever told her to believe the man she would end up with would be.

And what was even better, he still helped her figure out the mysteries of Shakespeare. Only this time, he'd lie there, with his head in her lap and read it to her. It was quite the most romantic thing she'd ever heard of.

They studied together and worked hard to earn their degrees. Because underneath the rosy glow of it all were the words she had come to live by.

'This is all very well, young lady, but don't forget. He won't marry you if you fail at the last hurdle. He'll want you to get a good hard working job for the first couple of years. Set you up for life. Then you can quit and have the children. Your mother wouldn't mind three grandchildren. Once you're married, I'll have words with the young man. Let him know, will I?' Her father had winked and spoken with heavy, ponderous joviality before he died.

One week before the end of university, she had a rather nasty shock.

She'd said she was going to the library. She had one exam left and while she knew it all backwards, a few hours at the library wouldn't hurt. But half way there, she changed her mind. These things happened. People sometimes realised there was such a thing as over studying and she just wanted to be in his arms for a few hours. It was hard to have the serious relationship they were having when she still lived at home.

So she turned round and went back to his place. He'd moved out of home. Mainly because his parents had left the district again and he'd chosen to stay. She'd hoped he'd stayed partly for her. But mainly she realised it was for the university. But she could pretend, just like all young women did, that in fact she was as central to his life as he was to hers. She just never bothered to ask him if this was true.

He lived in a group house ('not terribly hygienic and it doesn't speak of great prospects, dear, but he's young') not far from the university. It didn't take long to get back.

She didn't have a key, but they rarely locked up, and certainly not if someone was going to be home, which was nearly always. Someone slept late, or studied early, or had a party to get ready for. They all knew her, and she came and went as she pleased.

Only one housemate was home and he gave her a horrified look as she waltzed back in.

'I decided not to study, after all,' she explained, dumping her books beside the coffee table. 'It's a beautiful day, I know the work and I thought we'd go for a picnic.'

Well, she hadn't thought that at all, but it had popped into her head and sounded like a lovely idea. Plus, she always felt she needed to explain herself to his housemates. He laughed at it, but there she was. The idea that they may think she came back just to go to bed with her boyfriend made her skin burn. So she babbled along smiling like a crazy woman, until she was out of the lounge room and down the corridor.

She heard high girlish laughter and wondered which one of them had their girlfriend over.

His door was shut, with a red sock over the handle. She smiled, unhooking it. What a strange place to dump your sock. When they moved in together she'd have to take over the whole house. He'd need lots of help with laundry, cooking and such. He was lousy in the kitchen.

She cracked open the door and stepped through.

They didn't hear her. She stood there, mouth fallen open (yes, it does really happen, not just in books or movies. Shock could drop the jaw faster than a left jab) and fingers suddenly nerveless.

Her boy, so full of life and plans for their future, had another woman bent over the end of the bed. Her brain froze on the idea that just because she wouldn't 'do it' with her back to him, it in no way made it okay for him to 'do it' with someone else.

There was a grunt, an agonised moan or one full of ecstasy, she couldn't tell, from the woman and then it was over. Only then did they look up and realise they had an audience. She hoped he shrivelled up and fell off in shock. He certainly looked pole axed.

'But you're at the library,' was all he could say.

'Not any more. How do you do?' she replied, nodding at the woman, who just knelt there, unable to move.

There was a scene. But her mind was switched off and she could hardly hear him. The outcome was already assured.

She left.

As she walked out, she smiled rather vacantly at the housemate. He still sat in the lounge room, his face a picture of horror. He'd known, she realised: known the whole time she was prattling on about love and picnics and spending time together.

Her skin shivered with shame and humiliation.

Never again, she vowed, her heart freezing over. Her mother was right. They were all bastards. Her friends were right. They took your heart, that fragile crystal ball and held it in their hands. Then in one swoop, they crushed it to smithereens and swept the fine crystal dust into a bin – as an inconvenient mess they'd had to clear up.

She passed her exam; all of them, in fact. And on that last day of university, she sat with her friends and stared at the glamorous women who stalked past on legs two miles long, with three inch heels and shiny hair. Her ex, as she now had to concede he was, was going out with one of these glamazons.

'I'm ordinary,' she said out loud.

It tasted funny. Because for a brief moment, loving someone who had listened to her and laughed at her jokes and thought she was 'so special I hope I never lose you', had made her believe the lie.

He had made her believe that she wasn't ordinary at all; that for someone, she was extraordinary.

But the truth was it didn't make up for the fact that she'd been living a lie.

She rolled over on the sunburnt grass and in her mind she shredded the images that had played in her thoughts. Of emerald green lawns and white picket fences, with a golden dog that waved the fan of his tail in the faces of sunny children.

'Be glad you're ordinary,' advised her friend, staring at the engagement ring on her own finger. 'It's always good to know your place in the grand scheme of things.'

And she had to agree.

Now all she had to do was find it.

The new job

She'd finally sent off the application and received a reply. The interview process would determine if she was successful or not in the pursuit of a job in another department. A job full of well meaning gentlemen in suits who were too busy to play games and break hearts.

They were on missions. They had to have the proper wife, and hostess, for their plans. They needed a partner in this thing called life and she was going to be that partner.

Not for her was the rosy glow. She no longer thought in terms of having someone listen to her and think she was special. She just wanted someone to come along and make the other side of the picture appear. You know the one. They go out on Christmas cards. Mother, father and two picture perfect children who looked like a blend of their parents.

There would be a puppy. Not a golden dog. No, that dream was gone. It would be a spotty puppy, with personality, and perhaps a kitten. And she'd be happy. This man would hand her this happiness and these children, and all would be well. She would wipe all the images of the 'other man' out of her head once and for all. That hadn't been love. That had been an aberration and a devil, who had masqueraded as Love.

She knew better now.

So she went to the interview and smiled her way through a bunch of useless questions, knowing full well that it wouldn't help her to understand what was going to be expected of her. They always lied.

"It's a fast paced area. Lots of work and we like fresh dynamic people. You'll never be bored, that's for sure! We encourage a work life balance and flexible working hours. It's the public service. You understand.'

She smiled to herself.

Oh yes, she understood.

She'd be bored, she'd file, and she'd write endless reports for Ministers who never read them and for higher level bosses who lost them in the miles of paperwork on their desks. They'd get demands from Ministers who thought work life balance meant life balanced itself around work, which would lead to being in the office between eight in the morning and seven in the evening. That meant she'd have to leave home at seven and not get back until eight.

It was the sheer volume of work they hoped would alleviate the boredom, not realising that it was the repetition that slowly killed enthusiasm. And it was the sure knowledge that nearly everything you did had no meaning and didn't actually go anywhere that drained your will to bother.

But she didn't say any of that. She marvelled at how interesting it sounded and nodded her head sagely, saying how much she hated to be bored and being busy was 'quite the antidote to that, now, wasn't it?'

She got the job.

It was going to be more responsibility and her mother was getting older now. So she made arrangements and found her mother a lovely retirement village. This meant that she was finally living alone, for the first time without her parents to guide her.

She suffered many panic attacks over the course of months following that decision.

Her mother wasn't too happy about it, either.

But it was for a good cause. Her mother wanted grandchildren and she could see the new department had much more options in that side of things. But to be seen as a progressive young woman, she needed the space to work long hours, so her mother nobly gave up her role and went to the village. Her mother needed far more attention these days than she could give her.

'I promise I'll come by every weekend and every day I don't work too late. You'll not be alone. There are lots of activities and people to meet.'

Her mother groused about meeting new people at her age, but managed to be out playing bowls or something like that nearly every weekend she made a visit.

She kept chanting in her mind, 'I'm working hard. I'm sure I'm in the right job because there are a lot of high achieving suits in my department and not a lot of laughter. It will be only a matter of time before someone realises that I am the perfectly ordinary wife he's always wanted.'

Each time she chanted her little mantra, she got a pain in her stomach and her head would ache. But she kept at it because there was one thing she knew – she couldn't play pretend anymore. She was an adult now.

It had been a part of some fairytale, having that one person who thought she was so special. There was no need to be deluded anymore. She was ordinary, words were cheap, most men would say anything, and the amazing stories people told her were just that – stories. There wasn't anything more real about them than anything she could read in the glossy magazines, if she were to read glossy magazines, which she didn't.

No, reading material of that nature came later.

But she continued to play the game, because that's all it was. A game. She filed and wrote reports and watched and listened. One day, she knew someone would come along and see just how unexceptional she was and then they'd get married.

'Don't try to be something you aren't, dear.' Her mother had picked up where her father had left off. It was always reassuring to have loving advice from those who knew her best.

'There are a lot of frauds in the world. But when you get to know them, you'll realise that they weren't telling you the ugly truth. They were hiding it behind the image they like of themselves. Don't fret. That's their bad luck. You just stay true to everything your father and I have taught you. Don't imagine that your life will be any more interesting than someone else's, don't trust people at their word, do the job yourself if you want it done properly and wait for that special moment when you know you've found The One. Then he'll take care of the rest.'

She often wondered what The One was meant to do.

Ride in and bring sunshine, hopes and dreams trailing along in his wake, she supposed. Funny how nothing in life resembled the reality her parents had told her about.

The new job was full of new people to get to know. They had fascinating stories about what they planned to do in life and where they hoped to go on their holidays. When they came back from these holidays, they had endless pictures of sunny beaches and misty mountains they had hiked.

She wished she was bold enough to go on one of those types of holidays. In her holidays she brought her mother back from the retirement village and they pottered in the garden, planting everything she had forgotten to plant in the 'right season'.

There was one man who stopped past her desk nearly every day. But she didn't 'know'. She was waiting for that knowing her mother had promised would come along. How did she know he wasn't like the other one? The one who had ripped out her beating heart and examined it and found it too ordinary?

He was pleasant, friendly and sometimes very funny. There was a hint of mischief about him, as though his jokes could turn into something just a little more, if she was to encourage him.

She liked word play: the possibility of meaning something else behind ordinary sentences. It gave her hope, a very hidden hope not even really revealed to herself, that underneath her ordinariness, there was another layer. A layer that the magic of word play just might begin to find.

If she had the courage.

Which she didn't.

So she listened and frowned at any silly notions, and worried that time was passing her by. If she couldn't find someone to settle down with in this department there was no hope for her. All the women here found someone. There were dozens of someones floating around the office, just waiting to be found and treasured. She just had no idea of how to go about it.

University days were long gone. The act of experimenting seemed too draining and too daunting, and too humiliating. Ordinary people, she came to the conclusion, didn't run around getting all scientific about the art of love. Ordinary groups of people, of which she was very sure she was in, merely waited for The One to come along and all would be right in their world. The art of love was for those in the extraordinary group. She had to believe that. Or something was definitely wrong with her. And as no one wanted to believe that they were fundamentally unlovable, it was easier to think that she was merely... ordinary.

She wasn't too sure on the specifics. But she'd had enough ordinariness pumped into her mind through constant talks with her parents so she was sure she was on the right track.

So she took to ignoring the funny man who sat on the edge of her desk and told her almost, but not quite, risqué jokes. She took to looking around the office, wondering if any of the men there were as ordinary as she and would require a quite unexceptional bride before too long.

Mother was already making grandchild noises. There was the feeling in the air that time was not on the side of either of them. They were both 'getting on'.

'You'll be too old to have children or to cope with them soon, dear. And I won't last forever. It's bad enough your dear father never lived to see his grandchildren.'

There were always tears upon this statement. It gave her a queasy feeling. It was as though she could still disappoint him from the other side of the grave.

So she kept her eye out, in between filing and coffee, for the perfect man who wouldn't lie or cheat or steal her heart; but would grow old with her, content to be the ordinary couple who lived in a plain house and had three children. One for her father, he'd want it to be a boy. Named after him, of course.

But the new job wasn't going so well.

Oh, the work was. That was the easy part. No one could mess up filing or report writing after they'd done it for years. No, that wasn't the problem.

She was expected to achieve things, which was out of the ordinary in her experience of her roles. But not only that, she was expected to stand up and report on them in meetings: called meeting KPIs. They'd never used words like that in her last position (she discovered they were Key Performance Indicators). As far as she had been aware, there hadn't been any KPIs. Even the Minister didn't seem to know what they did. It had been a lovely black hole of a job where nothing was expected of you except to turn up. And write reports that reported on something. If in doubt make it up, had been the policy.

She'd written copious amounts of 'scoping papers'. Pluck out a topic, doddle around the internet (mainly Google and Wiki, as they were standard research bastions of the public servant) and then plop the information in a document. Make sure the document conformed to department specifics, had headers and footers and 'Bob's your Uncle'.

But now she had to show something. Anything, to prove that what she was contributing was ...well... actually contributing. That required thought and an idea behind her reports. It meant she had to follow up things. This all took time and suddenly a couple of years had gone past and she hadn't dated anyone.

She'd stayed behind her desk, laughing under her breath (so as not to encourage him and not to draw attention to the fact she was laughing in a serious place of work) at the rapidly becoming more risqué jokes of her companion and justifying her role at endless meetings to make sure that 'things were being done'.

Things *were* being done. Mostly she would send out a report, follow its slow progress through the department and then spend the following week writing a report to read out at the fortnightly meeting to explain why the other report had been necessary, where it had gone and why, and what it was hoping to achieve.

As far as she could tell, it didn't actually have to achieve what she hoped it would achieve. It just had to be seen to have a goal. Any goal would do. She often spent Wednesdays wracking her brain for a goal.

Thursdays every second week was the meeting. Then it was back to the drawing board, with a host of notes from the meeting, to write another report on definitive goals defined at the meeting.

All this took time and effort and thought. Her mother decided that she, the daughter, was going to be an old maid and destroy her mother's hopes and dreams of grandchildren. There was the undercurrent of 'you did this just to spite me, even though I sacrificed everything for you.'

She was surprised to notice how bitter her mother had become.

She started only spending Sundays at the village. It was easier on both of them that way.

Working hard at a career wasn't what she'd had planned. It had been a stepping stone in the grand scheme of things. A leap from which her life of happiness would come stemming from her newly made family.

She was fast becoming disillusioned. Even more so, when her joking friend up and married the woman seated in the desk behind her. It seemed he'd spent the whole time booming those jokes at her, trying to get the other woman's attention. He'd sat on the edge of her desk, because he liked the way his trousers would bunch and tighten over his thigh muscles, which he would flex by swinging his leg. While she'd believed it was for her, the whole time he'd been keeping his crafty eye on the other one and three years into the job she found them going off on their honeymoon.

There was no need to jump up and down, screaming that was meant to be *my* honeymoon. She realised men needed a bit more encouragement than a few laughs. But she was unsure of what stood between sleeping with them and a few laughs at silly jokes.

There appeared to be a whole world of difference, but her father and mother hadn't had any ideas or advice about that.

She started reading those glossy magazines. They had never been allowed in the house before, but she discovered she loved them.

They gave insight not only into the lives of people more glamorous than the ones she doted on at work. They also showed her just how wide that line between laughs and sex really was.

There was a whole new world out there.

The fine art of self pleasure

She'd listened to many people now. She still had the way of focusing all her attention on the one person in front of her and making sure she heard everything they said.

But now, instead of wondering what it was like for other people, she read about it. There were some topics she hadn't wanted to ask about. Though most women she knew had no trouble in discussing everything they did or didn't do in the bedroom, she was more interested in reading about it. That way, she found, she didn't go quite as red in the face as usual.

Even at twenty seven there was plenty left she hadn't experimented with. She found it strange that she had kept to the strictures her parents had laid down. She hadn't picked up a magazine apart from National Geographic in her life.

Now, her house resembled a newsstand. There was nothing sacred anymore, she came to the conclusion. Magazines went everywhere. Even into people's bedrooms, doctors and other private places.

She found the articles on various celebrities to be the worst. There was nothing in them except voyeurism. At least the other articles had some informational value. Studying what a celebrity did was... dirty. She didn't want her fantasies to have names, addresses and movie titles to their names. She wanted facts. Hard, cold, clinical facts that weren't inter-spliced with photos from a Hollywood boudoir. She watched a movie starring one of the celebs from her magazines. Once. It came as a nasty surprise to realise she could no longer see them in the same light.

There was such a thing, she thought, as over sharing. The world was full of over sharing. Couldn't they leave some of that for their next partner to find out on the night? Even the photos were over sharing.

45

But the information was a goldmine.

Two weeks after her passionate foray into the world of magazines, she went to a sex shop. She wished she could take a girlfriend with her. It was one of those experiences she didn't relish on her own. But the idea of telling anyone where she was off to in her lunch break didn't appeal. There was no one she could trust with the knowledge that not only did she not know all there was to know about bedroom antics, but she was off to discover it on her own.

So she went alone, even though she wished she wasn't.

Not only because she had come to the conclusion she was a bit of a prude – but mainly because it was something that should be shared. The first time you went into a shop based solely on the idea of pleasure, she had the notion it would have been nice to share the giggles with someone.

Because that was all she could do. Giggle.

Oh, that and buy herself the smallest and most ladylike vibrator she could find. Which was a lot harder than it sounds, because in the shop there were all shapes and sizes, but mainly ones that scared her stupid. They looked rather what she suspected a stallion would look like. But with studs and pebbles and all kinds of bits and pieces that moved, wiggled and made noises.

She held up a pair of handcuffs with pink fluffy bits dangling off it that came with the matching pink fluffy heels and see-through fluffy jacket. She wasn't one hundred percent sure of the point of the jacket, but there you go. It wasn't the sort of place you asked questions.

The sleazy guy behind the counter eyed her off over the top of a magazine, his black hair long and lank. He was wearing a fishnet T-shirt, had what looked like silver stakes through his nipples and a studded collar. There was a part of her that was so fascinated that if he hadn't been watching her so closely, she would have been staring at him.

She was sure the picture on the cover of his magazine was physically impossible, but she knew her experience was limited, so wasn't willing to bet on it.

Eventually, she gave up trying to understand half the things hanging on the walls, off coat hangers and strapped on various plastic models around the store. In a dark corner, tucked away almost as though ashamed because they lacked majestic size and terrifying shape, were discreet vibrators.

That's what they were called. Discreet. This nearly sent her into hysterics, as she failed to see how anything shaped like a penis that had three settings on the base could ever be construed as discreet. If it was ever found in her bedroom by her overly zealous cleaning mother, there would be nothing discreet about the explosion.

It was the hardest thing she'd done in her life – making her way back to the counter where sleazy counter guy gave her a leering wink and wafted Lynx aftershave all over her. The strangest thing was, after nearly an hour looking at the marvels of the modern sex life, the smell did weird things to her insides. She figured it was past time to be leaving, as the counter guy must have known the effect that Lynx could have after viewing mammoth penis' for an hour.

She only hoped that if anyone ever took him up on his silent offer, they wouldn't be disappointed. He had a lot to live up to.

Hiding the new found freedom and purchase in her car, she finished her day in the office. Seeing as funny man was still on his honeymoon and probably wouldn't be making an appearance on her desk any time once he did get back, the afternoon dragged.

This, she tried to convince herself, had something to do with the fact that the report she was working on was dull and boring. Underneath that false excuse was the idea that her new purchase was languishing in the boot of her car less than two hundred metres away and home time was a couple of hours away.

It felt like light years.

Eventually it dawned on her. She was a public servant. Flex time was exactly for such occasions as having a vibrator in your car neatly wrapped in discreet brown packaging, waiting patiently for you to get home.

'I've got to get home early today. Got a date,' she said to her supervisor, knowing full well that five forty five wasn't early in anyone's books except for him.

This new job was just chockfull of work/life balance.

He raised his eyebrows, but didn't comment. The fact she'd never had a date before, or ever spoken of anything remotely personal in the time she'd been there, might have something to do with his surprise.

Though it was slightly less daunting to be at home sitting on your own bed, nevertheless she found herself dissolving into giggles as she unwrapped her purchase. Batteries were not included, but she had lots at home.

Her father had instilled in her the need to always have a good array of batteries in the house.

'There are torches in case of a blackout. You know how you get when it's dark. You can never have too many torch-sized batteries. Things tend to go flat just when you need them the most.'

This salient piece of information floated into her head as she placed the two AAA batteries needed for operation into the vibrator. This of course, led to more giggles. She wished she'd bought a second bottle of wine. The first one would only get her through the unwrapping and powering up stage at this rate.

'You need AA and AAA batteries, as well. You know your mother can't bear that stuff people call music these days. If you're going to play bee-pop then you'll need that walkman we bought you.'

When she asked about the AAA batteries he was stumped. There wasn't anything in the house that took them, but he wasn't defeated. To this day, there were packets of C size, and all the range of A batteries all around the house. She hadn't the heart to throw them away. Her mother was forever finding them in the strangest places when she did come over, and smiling. She decided that she'd have to go and buy a *lot* more packets, so her mother didn't notice they were disappearing.

Sipping her fourth glass of wine, she practiced with the switch.

It was a circular base that rotated. You simply rotated it as far round as you wished. Each time you moved it round further, the vibrator would ratchet up the speed. The sound would go up in semitones. By the time she'd rotated the base fully, the vibrator was making a high pitched buzzing sound and she was snorting wine out her nose.

'Not exactly romantic,' she commented to the kitten.

She'd found the kitten on the side of the road only the week before. Hoping it would help ease the loneliness of coming home to an empty house, she'd taken it to the vet. It became a 'he', who was deloused, neutered and vaccinated on the spot. She didn't want him to come home and transfer all his bugs to her carpet.

The kitten stalked the madly buzzing vibrator across the blankets. His fur was raised, so he resembled nothing more than an outraged ball of grey fluff.

'At least you aren't pink. I've had quite enough of pink fluff for one day.'

More than enough. She'd never been a fan of pink.

'But I agree. It doesn't engender the types of feelings I had hoped.'

Thinking about it, nothing made her feel like trying her new toy. She wondered if the sleazy guy behind the counter would take it back. Thinking about taking it back, made her think of buying it and the way he stared at her.

Then she hit on the one thing that was going to work.

Regretfully, she placed her purchase back into its wrappings and under the bed. Not tonight, dear. She didn't have a headache, but she wasn't filled with desire, either.

The following day simmering excitement kept leaking out of her. The supervisor gave her an odd look, but followed that with a smile. It was unusual, but she remembered she'd used a date for going home early. The idea of talking about it made her laugh. She smothered it into the palm of her hand. Never let it be said she was taking her job lightly.

For some reason, however, she noticed other people smiling or enjoying low-voiced conversations. She wondered if they'd always been doing this and she'd just not noticed. Being as she was, always 'working hard' at trying to prove that she was bright, ambitious but not too ambitious and certainly not so bright as to lessen the man in her life. It was a lot to be getting on with, so she hadn't noticed the low hum of human interaction all around her.

At lunch, instead of taking her sandwich to the park and sitting alone reading one of her magazines, she'd not brought lunch at all.

She grabbed some sushi rolls from one of the food court shops and headed into the men's section of a large department store. Feeling very daring, breaking all kinds of rules, she munched on the sushi roll (it didn't taste like salt, off fish or grass at all, thank you, father) and wandered up and down the display cabinets.

'Can I help you at all?' asked a fresh faced young man.

He smelt wonderful and she felt vaguely weak at the knees.

'I'm looking for the Lynx collection.'

Her voice was a bit squeaky. She'd never bought anything from the men's cosmetics section. It was a rather large leap, but there was nothing for it. Her discreet vibrator waited patiently at home for her to practice. She had to wipe out the giggles and the sound of the buzzing somehow. All hope rested on making her sense of smell so dominant in the upcoming situation she lost all ability to listen to anything.

'Great choice. I'm wearing a Lynx at the moment. Do you know what your man likes?' he asked.

She was stumped. Just how many were there? She hadn't anticipated questions. Just a quick in, sniff, grab the one that smelt like her sleazy counter guy and get out.

He led her to a showcase. It was overwhelming. Couldn't they make up their mind what the sexiest smell for a man was? They couldn't *all* bring out the animal in a man. Could they?

She smiled nervously at salesman guy.

'I'm not sure. Can I smell them all? Just until I find the one that's... familiar?'

She knew her face was slowly going red, but there was nothing for it. She'd never come back into this store for as long as she lived. That way, there was no way he'd ever recognise her and point her out to his mates. Guys did things like that. Just to make girls embarrassed.

'What? All of them?' He looked confused, but shrugged. She could almost see the thought pattern running through his head. Humour the crazy woman and just wait till I tell the guys about it tonight. She was dressed in a trouser suit, wore plain flat lace up shoes and wanted to *sniff* the collection.

She cringed inside.

This breaking out of her comfort zone, just as her favourite magazine had told her to, was not as easy as the smiling chick in the article had promised.

'Take a deep breath and believe in yourself. Know that you are the power in your life and you need no one to enjoy yourself. Take a hold of your courage and break free of your comfort zone. Eat new things. Go to new places. Try new positions with your partner or, girls; find that new position *all by yourself*. Give yourself permission to explore your body and feel how it responds. Know what you like and next time, don't be afraid to tell him. Or her!'

She remembered the passage by heart. She'd felt brave not bringing in a sandwich for lunch. Quite courageous ordering sushi rolls. Full of fearlessness walking into the store.

But somewhat lacking in the daring department now she was faced with a salesman and rows of men's aftershave and deodorant.

It took her the entire lunch break to decide on a scent that was guaranteed to tip her over the edge. It was hard to come to this conclusion with the salesman standing next to her. She couldn't concentrate properly.

All she wanted to do was stand there and drown in the smells. Drag lungful after lungful into her body, and wait to see if she started to vibrate - on the inside. If any of them made her go weak at the knees.

In her fear of his ridicule, she eventually just plucked a bottle off the shelf and thrust it into his hands.

'Now I remember. This one. This is his favourite,' she babbled.

Her only concern was getting out of the place. It wouldn't be until later that night she would find out it was exactly what she was looking for.

Another afternoon of struggling to hold in all the pieces of herself. Once upon a time, there hadn't been any fragments. She'd considered herself whole. One ordinary person, who followed the rules and lived a life out of the textbook.

She was still marvelling over the amazing sense of free-fall she was experiencing. There was a widening of her daily life and reading the extraordinary things in magazines, as she was now addicted to, was beginning to stretch things even more.

Sadly, she didn't notice there was more joy around her than she had ever expected. At this time, she was completely absorbed with the idea of her own freedoms. That others were already looking for theirs was not to occur to her until she turned thirty.

Finally, the day drew to a close. She hadn't pulled the 'date' card. Not twice. For some reason, she felt that no one would believe her. The idea that someone such as she could possibly have a date *two nights in a row* didn't seem feasible.

So, at seven, she made her way home, oscillating between the exhaustion of another mind numbing day trying to find a link between her section's main body of work and the report she was expected to write (there wasn't one) and the excitement bubbling in her chest. Her car smelt of Lynx. She'd sprayed some into the air when she got in. It was increasing her levels of excitement, but also creating bubbles of giggles.

At home she was greeted enthusiastically by the kitten. It was the homecoming she had been aiming for. Though she quite liked not living with her parents for once, coming home to a deserted house every day had started to become depressing. Having a cat was a wonderful antidote to this.

'Glad I'm home? So am I. And no, you won't be able to sleep on my bed tonight,' she informed the little kitten.

The image of him stalking the vibrator popped into her head. She couldn't have that again. She'd never get to the part where she worked out what worked best for her if she allowed the cat to distract her. Or maul her. He wasn't at the stage where he kept his claws to himself.

She settled the little fluff ball in front of a bowl of kibble, removed her jacket and turned on the gas. She needed something to eat before she went and had a shower. Something quick and light.

It wasn't long before the soft aroma of chicken in soy sauce with vegetables wafted out of the non-stick pan she'd placed on the gas stove top. Stir fries hadn't been a staple in the family home until recently.

Along with the desire to change so much more in her life, she'd started to experiment with her diet. At the start, she found herself eating plates full of congealed goo. But slowly she was finding the recipes where she could achieve something edible. They also needed to be quick and easy. She wasn't much of a cook and resented any time she had to spend in the kitchen. There were more important things to be going on with. Such as the enormous amount of reading she was doing.

Since discovering the magical world of magazines and the over-sharing abundance of people's opinions at such variance to the rules she had always lived her life by, she was devouring books by the dozen. She had also connected the house up to the internet.

This was a large step, by anyone's standards. She'd always had access to the internet at work. But it wasn't the same.

As a chronic rule follower, she'd never looked at anything that wasn't work related. She couldn't. It wasn't in her programming to bend things just that little bit. She didn't open email jokes, nor spend time wondering what else was out there. There was work to be done, no matter how stultifying - so she did it.

But trying new things and working on moving into the era in which she'd been born, had led her to install wireless connection and rapid internet. Each evening, she indulged in Googling a new site and reading everything that she could until she became cross-eyed.

She took out a glass and poured herself some wine. She cast the laptop a longing glance, but knew that if she was to turn it on, the entire evening would be consumed with other people's discoveries, not her own.

Sipping the wine, a cool crisp riesling, she filled a bowl with her chicken stir fry. She'd added a hefty amount of ginger this time, just to see how the taste would feel in her mouth. One fork full later and she smiled.

Ginger, she decided, was definitely on the must have list. She was constantly amazed at how many things she was adding to her 'must have' list. Things she would never have been game enough to try not that long ago.

The spicy, tangy and almost overwhelming pleasure of biting into a piece of grated ginger lying hidden in her vegetables, tickled her tongue. She licked her lips, gliding her tongue over their surface and allowing the residual ginger to bite into the small crack at the side of her mouth, which reminded her she needed to put more lip gloss on. There is nothing worse than dry lips, she had discovered in the past, when attempting to kiss someone. Lips should be firm, warm, soft and smooth.

The ginger continued to burn gently.

Eventually she'd eaten as much as she could. The last of the wine slid down her throat and she put everything into the dishwasher. It was an unheard of extravagance she'd indulged in a month after her mother moved out. Even now, every time she came back for a visit on the increasingly scant weekends she wasn't out doing something, her mother tutted about the dishwasher.

'I don't know how you can trust your dishes to that thing. What if it breaks them? How do you know they'll be as clean as if you washed them yourself? It must use a lot of water and power. It's such a waste. You live alone. It's not like you make all that many dishes to be washed.'

Her mother still liked to emphasise the fact she was alone in the three bedroom home. That there was no husband to guide her steps, or children to brighten her day.

Throwing these thoughts out of her mind, she undressed and stepped into the shower. She *did* live alone. So she allowed herself the luxury of two showers. One in the morning, to shake off any residual sleepiness and one in the evening. She hated to get into her crisp sheets with any of the day lingering on her body. It constantly surprised her how many of her friends showered in the morning, and of an evening, after a day of sweating, eating and shaking hands with Lord knew who, they just crawled into bed. They even made love, covered in the day's grime. It made her shudder.

So she showered and shaved her legs. Once she was dry, she smoothed moisturiser into her skin. She loved the way her legs felt straight after shaving: silky smooth and tingly. Almost as though the nerves knew they had barely escaped with their edges intact. One slip with the razor...

After the bathroom, she made her way to the bedroom in her softest underwear. She hadn't gone out and bought new underwear for this experience. For a moment she wished she had. Why not indulge completely? But the idea of putting things off, again, just to have silk underwear against her skin wasn't appealing. There was something to be said for getting on with things.

She climbed into bed and leaned over the side. In its box, with its new batteries and freed of all the wrapping, was her discreet vibrator. An errant chuckle escaped her lips. She reached over and took another sip of the recently filled wine glass.

Taking wine to bed, having something other than meat and three veg for dinner, eating sushi rolls for lunch and going to a sex shop. For a moment her brain fritzed and her heart rate doubled. There was an intense feeling of falling. She was trying far too many new things all at once. Then her eyes found the magazine, tossed onto the nightstand, still open on the article about believing in yourself. She took a deep breath. There was nothing to be afraid of; there was no one here except herself.

The art of self pleasure, her new guru had warned her, was not for the faint hearted. And it wasn't just for the bedroom, hence all the new things in her life: the sipping of wine, instead of gulping of water; the nibbling of new foods, instead of the stoic munching on the known.

'The act of self pleasure should be in everything that you do. Every part of your life can be a dance with pleasure. Allow yourself to think about all your daily routines and then – enjoy them! Add new twists to old favourites. Don't just eat in front of the telly every night. Only do it when exhaustion threatens. Take the time to sit and eat outside watching the stars come out overhead. Or savour each bite with a loved one. Share the candlelight and enjoy a glass of something sparkling. Know that it is safe and more than okay to explore all the longings of your heart. Know that it is easy enough to unbury those longings – if you listen for them.'

Slowly, she was finding she could listen. If she stayed still and quiet enough to hear. It was only through the prompting of these longings that she was able to lay back and fiddle with the end of her discreet vibrator, until it hummed with a gentle buzz. She slid one hand across to her breast, the other already at her inner thigh, the vibrator on low. There was plenty of time to find out if the outraged bee of full power was more to her liking.

The next morning she went to work with a bounce in her step. There were indeed things that were best explored on your own. Places so secret and so untamed, she felt her face flush even thinking about them. She had also found a passion for that outraged bee.

There were new things all around her on the way to work. She watched as a young woman and her man walked across the street in front of her car, sharing matching smiles full of secrets.

She felt like leaning out the window and telling them she understood, finally. There were secrets. There were whole universes of secrets right within her body. She felt she would be deafened with the new knowledge spinning around in her mind.

Work was a complete waste of time. This epiphany hit her as soon as the lift bell dinged. People were scurrying around, muted words on the latest crisis to hit the office. The Minister was demanding a full inquiry into a situation that wasn't meant to be on the list until next month. Everyone was caught short, which left a lot of tempers put out of place and people snapping at one another.

She could feel the tension in the air as she walked to her desk. The supervisor, who had smiled at her in bemusement when she'd claimed a date the other day, now scowled at her late appearance. She checked the clock. It was only five past eight. There was a voice in the back of her head that asked when it was okay for all this pressure to bring on indigestion? But the part of her that was starting to wake up to other possibilities went back to sleep.

Now wasn't the time for revolution.

PART III: THE MIDDLE BIT

Where the middle begins

It doesn't matter what plans you have for the future. It doesn't even really matter if you have worked hard for them every day. Something can come along and change the course of your life, in the blink of the eye. Your path could be there one minute and gone the next.

There are rules that everyone lives by. They can be imposed upon you, placed around you like a comforting blanket, or hardwired into the society within which you are born. These rules confine and restrict. There are very few that open and urge. Rules appear to be *made* to limit and constrict. They are put in place so as to narrow the options for those living within them.

Sometimes, however, someone comes along who feels the weight of these rules. They see the bars of their cage and wonder how things got to this point? They ponder what lies on the other side that isn't chaos and isn't anarchy, but is free choice and magic. They wonder if the fear implanted by generations that came before them is real. They wonder what lies on the other side that could possibly have led the rule makers to add more along the way. They speculate on the need for change and how to go about it. They work on making their lives 'fit' the hungers of what is on the inside; not the platitudes of what lies on the outside.

These people feel the freedom of wind on their faces, allow the wind to blow through their hearts and reach out with desire to what lies beyond.

She had read about them. They were visionaries and self help gurus who waffled on about making the most of yourself. They spoke of magic as if it happened. They spoke of the power of the mind and how that could be used to make the most amazing changes in one's life.

If only one had the courage to do so.

She read about how they had been stuck in high powered jobs, or had no job, or were homeless and afraid. How a monumental moment came along in their lives which helped them to see what they had been missing.

The answer. The riddle of life exposed.

She just didn't think it could be her. There was no magic bullet that would come flying into her life and make things different. It happened to other people, those with lives less ordinary. Perhaps they were special from the start; even though they all said it was a 'great event' or change that started them down the new path. But while she didn't believe it could apply to her, she read them.

She loved these books and websites. They offered hope and dreams.

Strangely, she was starting to dream again. She looked back at the secret longings of her heart and reread journals she had thought were long since destroyed or lost.

And most of all, through all this, she rediscovered her hatred of being ordinary.

It had been sitting there in her mind all this time. She had fought with it at university and thought she'd won. She'd looked around her and seen how ordinary she was, and spoken about it with her friends. This scientific research of the state of the ordinary had led her to believe it was okay and she had accepted that yes, she was going to live this life under the radar.

But as she started to make some changes; as she played with new things and experimented with the delightful and somewhat clandestine art of self pleasure in all aspects of her life, she discovered the lie.

Underneath the concrete she had paved over her heart there lay the secret truth. She still loathed the idea of being ordinary. Of being labelled as anything, of not allowing the dream to flourish. Of not even knowing what the dream was.

The quiet voice in the back of her mind dared to ask:

What makes you so sure you are ordinary? Just because your father told you not to expect anything in life to go your way because ordinary people have to work hard at everything? What makes you believe *he was right?*

These words would play around in her mind when she'd wake at three a.m. Why was it, she often wondered, that the big things in life came back to haunt you at three in the morning? Couldn't they appear to weigh on your mind during the day?

But no, her secrets, hopes and dreams; her fears and horrors; and worst of all, her shames and guilts; would all come into her mind when the night was settled around her like a cloak. She would stare up at the ceiling that she couldn't see and wonder at the things she had done and believed in. And that still, small voice in her head would tell her there was something else out there. She could have it all.

If only she believed.

Only - it never mentioned what it was she was meant to believe in.

That would have helped, given her a path of sorts. The kernel of an idea of what it was she was supposed to have faith in.

Her parents had taken her to church as a young child. They had reared her as God fearing and obsessed with the concepts of Heaven and Hell. The eternal night of fire and brimstone that would eat away at her and she'd live there forever.

When she was very little she'd wake screaming in the night - only on Sunday nights. After another feisty sermon on how depraved and full of sin the human being was and how she'd end up burning in Hell if she ever did these things: the list was endless in her childlike mind. She did half of them before breakfast. At least, in her mind she did. And the man behind the pulpit assured them all that God was watching everything they did and said and thought. Even their thoughts could lead to Hell.

She was destined to burn.

It seemed a little unfair to the teenager who went slowly and unwillingly to church every Sunday. She hadn't actually acted on any of these thoughts. They just lingered in her rebellious teenage brain like a fine mist shrouding her personality.

Then she grew up and never went back to church, but the idea of a Heaven and Hell lingered, and she would wake at three in the morning sweating with the fear that God was counting up all the things she'd done wrong and one day she'd have to pay. The great cosmic scales would be against her. The scientific experimenting in university with bodies and lovers, and the discreet vibrator in her bedside drawer... she knew those scales weren't tilted on her side.

So reading about people who went on to overcome the fears and insecurities that their upbringing had instilled in them was somehow very uplifting; even if she thought of them mainly as fiction.

It was around this time, nearly thirty by now, her mother passed away. It wasn't an easy death and she wasn't let off without some of her mother's bitterness at life in general and her in particular.

'I never did get any grandchildren. You knew it was the hope of my life, to have them to guide and watch over. And yet you've made no effort at all to settle down. Your father would be so upset,' were her mother's last words to her.

She didn't try to explain that finding the perfect partner wasn't as easy as they had led her to believe.

Not with all the rules and guidance they had to add, anyway.

How to find a man who would: not make unreasonable demands, take out the garbage, not get sweaty palms, not ask for a kiss on the first date, not want to take her home – but still find her attractive, had a very good job with good prospects, wouldn't mind that she had a good education and good job, but happy for her to give it all up once the children came. This man was meant to take care of her and provide in some way small portions of happiness that she would be content to remember and live on for all the days of her life.

She patted her mother's hand and didn't tell her, 'If I spent all my time trying to find someone who fit any or all of your stupid rules, then is it little wonder I am alone? You never helped me to think of myself as important and as worthy of this man. Is it any wonder he never thought so either?'

She wanted to tell her mother that she had taught her daughter to distrust what people said, distrust men in general, distrust her own gut reactions and yet, expected her to trust someone with the remains of her life. She sat there with her mother until she passed away and not once did she open her mouth and explain the choices her mother had made weren't the ones that would help her daughter. That in this life, this new life where people could pick and choose how they felt and what they did, rigid rules were being tossed out the window and a fresh breeze of change was taking their place.

She didn't mention that slowly over time the image of bonnie children holding onto her hand as they all crossed the road had faded. The idea of a puppy, a handkerchief garden and a handsome dark haired husband had disappeared inside walls of disappointment. Such was the dominance of her parent's wishes; she'd only had moments to consider her own. And one of those hidden and buried ideas was a vague feeling she didn't even want the image they'd given her.

It was heresy, she knew. Everyone was meant to want children. She'd been brought up to believe in the concept of family so strongly, it made her palms sweat and her stomach churn when she even imagined there was another possibility: a life out there without the responsibility of a husband and three children. Because that was the number her father had told her was sensible. One son for her husband, one daughter for her and one extra as a special treat for all concerned, even the country, perhaps.

But she'd been watching her friends and their families. The hours spent with their children and the nappies, the washing, the cooking, the sniffles, the demands and the husbands who went out to play golf on the weekends and left the wife to do it all. She didn't know what else a life could look like, but she was starting to believe she should try.

One girlfriend's husband had decided he wanted six kids. Her friend wasn't all that strong, but she didn't know how to say to her husband that six was a bit too much. She was bogged down in brats knee deep and longed for freedom.

Sitting there watching her mother dying, she wondered how her friend was doing. It had been so long since they had spoken. She had given up calling because all her friend spoke of were children, nappies and how fast they were learning to read, speak, walk, crawl.

She wasn't interested in other people's children. She hoped this didn't make her unnatural, or that her friends would notice her indifference. But they were leaching the idea of children of her own, right out of her.

These were thoughts she could never explore with her mother. One set of thoughts, like so many others, that her mother wouldn't understand because they were so foreign. She bit her lip and waited for her mother's hand to slacken in her own, then she made arrangements for the funeral.

This time, she was too numb to think past the arrangements. She was now an orphan. She had no living relatives and no one else to lean on.

Five weeks after her mother died, she got the flu.

It was little wonder, really. Everyone told her she should have taken more time off when her mother died. But it was budget time, after the end of the financial year and she had reports to write and a Minister to placate. She couldn't afford to take too much time off.

Just goes to show, she thought later, she was meant to be at home. The flu knocked her around and she ended up calling in sick for the week.

Lying curled up on her bed she didn't even feel up to any of her new self pleasuring exercises.

She didn't sip wine, savour food, or buzz with the Bee, as she had started calling her vibrator, for the lack of anything else discreet to call it.

She lay there, feeling like death was trying to claw its way into her life and take it over. The aches in her bones reminded her of the pain her mother had warned her about when she got arthritis. But luckily she knew this pain would go, unlike the arthritis.

Eventually, she could get up and around again. It was time, she thought, to make her way out into the garden.

Winter had let go and spring was making an appearance. There were daffodils and sweet smelling flowers dotting the garden beds. She hadn't paid that much attention to them in a long while, but they faithfully gave forth a beautiful array, as though to remind her they were there.

It was warmer than she'd being expecting. But that could have been, she realised, the residual effects of the flu, the antibiotics for the chest infection that had taken over, or the fever she hadn't even known was hiding in her body.

She hoped it wasn't a strong fever.

Whatever the reason, she stripped off all her clothes, feeling remarkably free and living on the edge by doing so. The house she had grown up in had a fully enclosed backyard and her neighbours would not only have had to be at home (which they were not) but also approximately eight feet tall to see over the fence and hedge. So she wasn't too worried about that, but still there was a definite feeling of walking on the wild side, wandering naked around her backyard.

She bent to kiss bobbing flower heads and stroke leaves unfurling in the spring warmth. It was a new experience; this actually caring what was in her garden.

With a jolt, she realised it really was her garden.

Both her parents were gone and there was no one to tell her how to order things, what plants to put where, and what it should look like.

This haphazard spattering of colour, of plants that had survived her rather limited gardening skills, was all hers to enjoy.

After a good half hour walking around murmuring to the flowers and plucking random weeds from beds of poppies and petunias, she settled herself under her favourite tree.

It was a large gum tree. Her father had hated that tree. It threatened the neatness of his lawns and her mother's carefully tended gardens. It threw leaves at them, dropped the occasional branch and towered over everything else.

The only reason they had it was the place came with it already firmly established. And they didn't get rid of it because it would have cost a fortune to get someone to come in, find a way around the house, and lop it safely. Her father had decided they would eventually sell the house and it would become someone else's problem.

They had never sold the house.

So she curled herself up under the tree, its massive branches arching above her. They were smooth and creamy and twisted in architectural beauty. The grass prickled her naked bottom, but she merely curled up her legs and sat on them. She didn't want to go back inside, not just yet.

Leaning back, she put her bare back against the smooth skin of the tree. It was cool and firm, but warmed where she touched it. She looked up into the waving branches overhead and her mind slipped away.

The infection may have been on the wane in her system, but she was still more relaxed than she'd ever felt before.

Looking up at the sky, filtered through branches and gum leaves, she wondered how God had allowed the world to get so messed up. Didn't She realise things were going to Hell in a hand basket? She squinted up through the leaves, the sunlight making strange spots before her eyes.

The trouble was there were too many people running around mucking up the world. They all wanted to have everything and they all had such wildly different ideas of what 'everything' was and how to get it. They were running around, grabbing at what was offered and sometimes taking what wasn't.

She wondered why she felt so disconnected with her life. Was it because she was ordinary? Or perhaps it was because she wasn't and only thought she was?

This sort of thinking went round and round in her mind. It spun a little and she had to agree, perhaps the infection, fever and antibiotics weren't quite all out of her system.

'The thing is,' she said to herself, 'I feel there are things I need to be doing, but I can't think of what they are. I feel so out of control, even when I am in control of everything in my life.'

She could hear the lie in that statement even as she said it. She couldn't control many things about her life, but she liked to pretend she could. It was the illusion of control that was so... comforting.

'Sometimes, I feel as though my life has been hijacked and I am riding a runaway car, my foot not quite on the gas or on the brake. I don't think this is how things are meant to be, but how does one go about changing them? I don't suppose it's easy to have a life changing event. You can't manufacture one.'

She realised what she wanted was that epiphany her favourite authors spoke of. They hadn't had much idea of what they were doing and where they were going, either. Until that one special moment had happened and suddenly they had the Keys to the Kingdom.

They *knew*.

They had the answers and knew where they were headed and what they were meant to be doing here.

She wanted some of that knowing. Some of what they spoke about. The certainty they wrote of. The way their words would leap off the page and speak to her in ways she never thought was possible. There was power there and she longed for it.

With her eyes half shut, she wished with all her might that she understand – anything.

'You need to be more like me.'

She sat up, dislodging the kitten who had settled in her naked lap. He screeched his displeasure and scattered, fur stiff with his feelings.

There was nothing and no one there.

She leaned back against the tree and sighed. If there was no one there and she was hearing voices, she was more ill than she thought possible.

'How do I move on? What do I do next?' she asked the air.

'You need to be more like me. Be tree,' came the response.

She realised she wasn't hearing this response out loud, so much as with a deep knowing in her chest. Like the voice was speaking in her heart.

The idea of being tree was faintly appealing, so she closed her eyes and concentrated on the feeling on her back. The strength and the smooth power of the tree she leaned against.

'What does it mean to be tree?' she asked herself.

'I bend with the wind; I do not break. I change with the seasons; I do not fight them. I stretch down low and grip the earth for balance, but I reach up high and touch the universe. I am strength and solidity, the fragile birth of new leaves, with the toughness of forever. I praise the sun for its part in life. I listen to the music of the stars and the songs of summer. I grow. My whole life is about growth. I am put here for no other reason than to grow. Upwards and onwards, to grow and change and be tree. So, be like me.'

She thought about this extraordinary conversation.

There was a small part of her mind that told her this was ridiculous and people didn't actually speak with trees. Well they might, but trees weren't in the habit of responding.

Somehow this logic seemed terribly irrelevant, or even outrageous. Of course people could speak to trees, her non-logic brain explained. Most of them just never chose to hear what the tree had to say to them.

As with most things, it was a one way conversation. People wouldn't listen. They would just sit there and wait for the next opportunity to hear themselves talk. They didn't have the patience to listen. And if they did; they didn't *hear*.

This came to her through her heart. It was like listening to something underwater, filtered in some way, but still clear. She could hear with every fibre of her being. The fever that had seeped through her system had allowed the usual distractions and mental chatter to be still. And in the silence was left a conversation she would never forget.

'What am I meant to be doing? Is this all there is for me in life? Will someone come along and deliver me my happiness? What is the next step everyone keeps talking about? Am I... ordinary?'

Her mind nearly didn't finish that last question. There was a part of her that didn't want to know the answer. Still stuck on her fear that she would die so ordinary no one would ever understand what went on in her mind, or care for that matter, she didn't know if she wanted the answer. But somehow, it was less threatening to be having this conversation with a tree than with someone more human. So she asked.

There was silence for a moment. The air itself paused, not stirring her hair.

Then the tree above her moved, shrugging its massive branches as though drawing breath, or sighing.

'You have many questions. So much chatter. There is no stillness. Be like tree before the storm. Take your time. Find your passion and your heart. Listen to them. Learn that the only things that are real and constant are Love and Change. Move and grow and think and speak. It is all change and brings about more change. But do it with Love.'

She shook her head.

'Nothing can be that easy.'

It was denial. Life wasn't meant to be easy and wasn't fair and was harsh. These were things that had stuck with her throughout her childhood. Even more, what had come from her heart hardly even began to scrape the surface of the questions.

'Be more clear.' There. The ball was in its court now.

In the back of her mind, she could see logic brain stepping forward, coughing politely.

'You're talking to a tree,' logic brain reminded her gently; talking as though she was incredibly slow. 'You do realise that trees aren't real. Well, they're real, but they don't speak. It's not logical.'

Well, no. She knew that. But she was quite happy to take a vacation away from logic, so she smiled and held it out a toy, a bright shiny toy. Minds and logic brains loved riddles; things to play with, to distract themselves with while you go right on having foreign correspondences.

'If trees can't talk, then what am I talking to?' she gently inquired of logic brain.

It sat down in the corner of her mind and started to pull apart the logic of her question. While it was busy doing that, she was free to continue her highly irregular conversation with the old gum tree that her father had hated so much.

She tilted her head as far back as she could. The top of her head was now resting on the bark of the tree. Her eyes stared upwards and for a crazy moment, the world tilted on its axis. She was seeing things from a completely different angle. All upside down and strained. There was pressure on her throat muscles from the strange position she held her head.

But there was something inside of her that said this was a good thing. That sometimes, seeing things in a new way was as simple as *seeing things in a new way.* And the best way to do that was to change your position.

'You know,' she spoke out loud just to hear her own voice and know that she wasn't going mad, 'you look very weird upside down like this.'

It wasn't the politest conversational gambit, but she was still a little spun out to realise she was listening to a tree talk.

'You walk around on two poles, talking from a hole in your face, listening but never really *hearing,* and you call a tree weird?'

It had a point. But it still hadn't answered all her questions.

By now she was getting a little cold and drowsy. Her skin was cool to the touch and the sun was moving across the sky, heralding the middle of the afternoon. Soon, it would be too cold to sit outside naked. Not knowing if she would ever be in a position to speak to the gum tree again, she wanted it to tell her the future.

'I really need you to answer all my questions.'

'You are so impatient. But never ordinary.'

Her chin sank down onto her chest. The tightness she had never realised she had, that was clutching her heart and constricting her breath, relaxed. One lone tear ran down the side of her nose.

She wasn't ordinary.

She wasn't ordinary. She *wasn't* ordinary. She wasn't *ordinary.*

No matter what way she looked at it, the statement stayed the same.

Okay, so she was only going on the say-so of a tree. But it felt good. As though there really was magic and the wicked witch had been slain.

'There is nothing ordinary in this world. There are only perceptions and intent. You have perceived yourself as ordinary for too long. So now go forward knowing that you are free of this misconception. You are joy and love and peace and magic, all in one. There is no such thing as ordinary. For all of you are wonderful beings of incredible power and possibility. Only, you never allow yourselves to see your own magnificence.'

She glanced down at herself.

If a tree could see anything magnificent about being too thin, having irregular bones sticking out all over the place and matted hair, then it was as delusional as she was starting to feel. Losing weight when you have the flu could be a blessing – she now had hip bones, but on the down side, they weren't pretty hip bones like you'd see on a model.

She wondered if the men in little white coats would soon appear and lead her off to a secluded mansion where they fed the patients 'vitamin' pills and hoped to rehabilitate them.

'What makes you think you are crazy?'

It had something to do with hearing remarks made by a tree, but she kept that little conversational gem to herself. Though if it knew she was thinking she was mad, then it possibly knew everything she was thinking.

'Of course I do. We are all connected. All one.'

'I'm a tree?' She found that a bit hard to believe. She held out her hand and turned it one way, than another. Nope, it didn't resemble bark. It was still very hand-like.

'You are energy. You, me, there is nothing you are not. What is the next step, you ask? Will someone come along and bring my happiness in their wake? Why should they? For if you allow someone else to provide you the happiness you crave, then it is a simple thing for them to take it away again. Do not give them this power. For all the power of the universe is yours. Take it and make your own happiness. You keep the universe inside of you. Provide for *yourself*. Focus on bringing the light of love and universal energy to yourself, and the next step will come to you. Do not feel that to do this will make you selfish. It will make you self *focused*.'

She wondered what the difference could be. They both sounded the complete opposite of all those Sunday lectures.

'The difference is the intent. Bring in the love you wish to have, and the happiness you crave, to your own life and know that in doing so, you are providing the world with a new source of all these things. That source is you. While you doubt; while you have no faith and do nothing to help your own light shine, you are denying the world the beauty that is you.'

She snorted. She couldn't help it. The beauty that was her? Mousey and brown and ordinary. It was her lot in life. No half feverish conversation with a gum tree was going to change all that.

Dragging herself up, she made her way inside. The logic brain inside needed to taste the ordinariness of her life once more. To see that it was only in books that magic happened. So she went in, to reread her books on the miracles that saved and changed the lives of others. There was no denying that it wasn't every day trees spoke to you. But a part of her wasn't ready to acknowledge the importance of what had been going on. That part wanted her to go back to bed, back to sleep and dream the dreams of the perfectly ordinary.

It's a lot safer to accept things as they are. Logic brain had given up trying to decipher the question she had posed to keep it quiet, and come back to the front of her mind.

Don't do anything out of the ordinary. You'll be cast off and people will think you're a crackpot. You don't talk to trees; you work hard and look for someone to father those children your mother wanted. You don't rock the boat, you don't think about what might be 'out there' and you certainly don't believe in a universe that thinks and speaks and has energy all of its own.

You believe in Heaven and Hell.

There. She wondered why logic brain sounded panicked, but put that to one side. The flu had tired her and she wasn't ready to face anything else that day.

Taking the kitten up in her arms, she went back to bed. It seemed... safest somehow. Her befuddled mind couldn't cope with the idea that something had happened. Something powerful and magical and strange that was about to transform everything she had ever known.

A pillow, a good book, and a nap were infinitely more doable.

Learning to Listen

Going back to work was a disheartening experience. She'd almost come to the conclusion it had been a dream: the getting up, putting on the power suit, driving through traffic, finding a parking space and logging on. Facing miles of research because she was behind and needed to get up to speed as fast as possible so she could write a new report; she had lost the heart for the act, the pretence that it mattered at all. That anything she did in the office would make the least amount of difference in the overall picture of the state of the nation. She felt as though some sort of fog had been lifted. That the blindfolds of her life were being taken away. And what she was left with was very dissatisfying indeed.

She sat at her desk and listened.

There was a conversational hum in the office. It sounded like sandpaper rubbing at a blackboard. It grated against the solitude and quiet she'd had the past week. It sounded nothing like the wind rushing through the trees, the gentle bobbling of flowers; nor like the heart-to-heart she'd had with the gum tree.

She sat and looked around.

There were people everywhere going about their daily lives and doing the things they had done a thousand times before. They wore tight smiles and desperate eyes. How could she never have noticed the strait-jacket that was her life until now?

Funnily, she couldn't see the epiphany as it was happening. There was no warning that life was about to take a rather large leap away from the tracks she was so sure of. Later, she would wonder if all the people who come to realise there is magic in all things didn't see the changes as they occurred. Did it take hindsight? Did it take time to see the change of course?

But that day, all she could see was the discontentment of her own Soul.

71

Her Soul had had a moment to come alive. And now she was trying to put it back in the box that she had been comfortable with. There were reports to write and she knew that no one else would get them done. It was up to her.

The captive bird inside her chest fluttered, alarmed. One chance to change her life and she was going to go back to sleep.

Her heart pounded faster. She felt her palms go sweaty and her vision dimmed. Perhaps she had come back to work a little soon? She had a rule for this. Her brain fumbled around trying to find her father's words in the silence.

'Don't take too much time off. Ever. You know what they say.'

She hadn't known what 'they' had to say, but then again, she never seemed to and her father was always delighted to inform her.

'If you take too much time off, they'll find someone else who can do the job. They'll realise no one is irreplaceable and you'll find yourself looking for another job. Always turn up. I once went to the office even though I'd had an operation two days before. They were amazed; called me a 'keeper'. That sort of dedication is always appreciated and noted.'

She didn't think her father would understand the grindstone of the government. It not only didn't appreciate, it didn't even notice. People came and went and did their job (or didn't, if something better came along) and things went on. Nothing stopped the grinding momentum of the governmental machine. No one was noted. They were numbered.

Little human touches were dealt out every day between colleagues, because if they didn't try to find some sort of connection amongst their fellow employees, then they would be lost in the system forever.

She wondered if she could just get up and walk out. If there was a rule for or against this situation: knowing that nothing was right and she felt displaced.

The fluttering in her chest lessened. Non-logic brain said the more she questioned the 'fit' of her circumstances, the better she'd feel. It made no sense to her, but she was ready to try anything. Anything to prevent the fluttering from coming back and the sense of vertigo when she looked at her workload.

'I must go home,' she said to her supervisor. 'I can't stay. I'm not well.'

He looked at her with a slight frown.

'We've got to get this brief done before ten. Can't you stick around 'til then? If you didn't think you could make it, you shouldn't have come at all. But now you're here, we need you.'

Her hands felt slick with sweat. She knew her face was shiny with it.

'Just till ten. Then I have to go. I don't want to make everyone else ill.'

'God, no. Stay put, write the report and then go home. The last thing we need is anyone else off sick. And this time, don't come back until you're one hundred percent.'

One hundred percent. That sounded a long way off. But the nerves that made her sweat settled down. She had two hours, then she was free. Anyone can cope for two hours.

Driving home, she passed the department store where she had bought the Lynx. She slowed down, trying to peer inside, to see if the young man was still there. It wasn't as though it mattered. But somehow, the idea of a connection with someone outside the office felt good.

It took longer to get home than usual. She felt as though she was driving through treacle. Her body moved slower than she thought possible. Her brain was foggy, like cotton wool. Her movements restricted, weighted.

The kitten was curled up in a patch of sunlight on the couch. He leaped up in shock to see her come home so soon. He rushed over to crawl up her trouser suited leg. The greeting made her feel more grounded and somehow more present.

'I know. I should be at work. But I can't seem to think clearly,' she told the kitten.

She glanced out at the backyard. The gum tree waved at her in the slight breeze. She put the kitten down.

'I know who is to blame for all this,' she said, grimly, marching out to the backyard.

Nothing was wrong until she'd spoken to that tree. She knew this wasn't true, that the truth lay in the fact she was adrift and had no idea of what to do. But she didn't want to face the truth just then. She wanted to point the finger, and the blame, at something, or someone else. Seeing as her options were limited, she marched up to the trunk of the tree and slapped it.

'There. How dare you get into my head? Talk to me as though you know my mind? Make me feel...' She stopped.

How did she feel? Now she was home, away from the sandpaper rasp of the office and the distinct feeling that her clothes (office) no longer fit? As soon as she had touched the ground in the yard the sense of hopelessness and overwhelm disappeared, it was temper that had carried her the rest of the way.

That and the fearful thought she was going mad.

She placed her hand on the trunk, with more reverence and tenderness. It wasn't the tree's fault she was crazy. Maybe the flu had unbalanced her mind.

The touch was soothing. The contact cleared the remains of her disjointedness away.

'You are not being tree. You have allowed the world to upset you and snap you like a twig.'

She leaned her brow against the smooth coolness.

'The world doesn't work like you think. I can't just do what I wish to. I can't forget the plans and rules laid down for me. I can't walk away from all that I am, and have been, and bend like that.'

There was a tinge of frustration in her voice.

She remembered reading in one of her self help books that the only thing in life is to do the things that you love. That led to more love and more doing and then before you knew it, you were the love. She had greedily gulped it all in.

Now, she wasn't so sure.

Growing up, she knew that you had to work hard and that to do this, you needed to find the job that made you feel... hard. If you enjoyed it too much, didn't that mean it wasn't work?

How did one get by on doing what made them joyful?

There was a flicker in her mind. How does one find out what *made* you joyful, was more the question.

'You spend time with yourself and learn to listen to your heart and your dreams, rather than the voices of others.' The tree, the essence of whatever it was she was communing with, was plucking her thoughts and feelings straight out of her head. She no longer needed to articulate them.

'You have forgotten what it is like to dream. The older you became, the more detached you became to the real you, the 'you' who dreamt of all the things that could happen. That thought magic was possible and all of life was abundant with things loved and needed. You lay back on the grass here and shaped a future that glowed. But slowly over time that future disappeared, as you allowed the world to stomp it out of you.

'You came to believe that life is meant to be hard; you have to struggle for what you want because that is how the world perceives it. You took those dreams and papered over the writing on the walls of your mind and buried it all so deeply.

'Yet the yearnings of a heart untapped will not go away. They sit inside of you and make you ache with them. They dance in your mind's eye and play tricks on you. Your dreams know what you could be doing. They listen to the silence of your soul and know you were once Joy personified. They'll lead you to places you always dreamed of.'

She clutched the trunk of the tree and wept tears of a lifetime.

Her dreams of a life far less ordinary than the one she was living: the dream that had settled into the greyness of working hard, of listening to others and not following her own heart and making her own choices.

She settled onto the ground once more.

Gone was the fear that she was listening to madness. If this was madness, she decided, let it swamp her. Let her be out of her mind and hunt those dreams down.

'I once thought that I could be the princess of my world. I remember lying on the grass just over there,' she pointed to the half dead patch of lawn that she continually forgot to water. The shameful neglect made her eyes burn.

'I would watch the clouds and they would tell me their story. They would tell me they went everywhere and saw everyone and made funny pictures so children would laugh. They showed me pictures of things that could come to be, if I chose to let them. They showed me magic in the sky.'

She felt sad that she had forgotten to look at the clouds in a very long time. Except in exasperation when it seemed like rain was coming and she wanted the sun.

'I believed that anything was possible, if I made it so. I knew my heart wanted to connect with people and trust what they were showing me was what they really were.'

She half thought for a second she could hear her father's voice telling her that people were never what they seemed and were always to be distrusted. She managed to quash him.

People were just people. They weren't any more or less than how they presented themselves. If they lied long enough, they became that lie. So in the search of who they were, it was the truth.

Was that why she had always sat with people and listened? Wanting to know what made them who they were and how they were? Because as a young girl, she had looked up into the heavens and thought – wouldn't it be nice to know people? To have a connection? To feel that extraordinary connection with more than one person, because in the reality of things, people are all wanting the same things: to feel heard and to be loved.

She smiled. It seemed very simple. And perhaps it was.

'It is simple,' came the echo in her heart.

'You have managed to make it so complicated because you have forgotten so much of what you were as a child. That child, all children, given the chance, are open, aware and loving. You were far more alive as a child than you are now. But you can always come back to life. Just choose to be free. Choose to live again and breathe life into those dreams.

'Know that your gift of knowing people is not a lie. Take that gift and apply it in all that you do. Go out there and be true. Take your heart and your soul and make them one. Be the soul of love and don't shut out the voice inside.'

Once more she smiled. There was little chance she would be shutting the voice away. It came so strongly from her mind and heart she wondered at how she had never heard it before.

It was a deafening roar; an avalanche of sound and feeling. It was the defining moment.

Her head jerked up.

Yes. This was it: The Moment. The point of change upon which hinged the crucial Next Step. She could choose to stop listening. To dim the roar of escaped feeling. And once more be trapped within her preconceptions and limitations.

Or she could choose to be brave, to admit that something was missing. That all the rules and ideas planted in her head by others were not the rules she wished to live by anymore. It was time to start making her own choices. The ones based on the feelings on the inside.

She closed her eyes and looked deeply into her heart.

76

The feeling of being out of control started to melt away. The idea that the world was a big, bad and scary place she had to hide from lifted. In its place, she could see the stars.

Inside of her was the universe.

She spread herself out on the lawn, opened her eyes and stared down into the clouds.

Looking at the world this way made her realised she had been living a very small life. It was a life defined by rules others had given her. Rules that made their lives as barren and empty as hers had become.

There were no dreams in the world of rules. There were constructs and rigid ideals. In the creative spaces that were opening up on the inside she could feel something fluid moving in her chest. It was wide and deep and never stopped moving. It was the flow of her mind and she dived right in.

She'd felt safe in her small world. Safe, but cramped. But the cramping had been slowly disappearing because she had made herself small enough to fit, shrivelled, in fact. Deep inside, the idea that life held more, had continued to try to escape. Life had presented her with ways to explore the universe inside, but she had never made the connection.

So sure that all the rules were there to guide her when her steps faltered, she had never made the jump and sought out experiences for herself. Her minor experimentation in university had been controlled, based on the idea that people couldn't be trusted and she had to be scientific in her exploration of love, and it had been based in fear.

It hadn't really had anything to do with love at all.

The more she had conformed, the smaller and tighter her world had become. It had shrunk to fit the confines of her routines. And those had been put in place by others.

She realised that instead of exploring life and taking large bites of it, she had been content to nibble the leftovers, the crumbs of other people's dreams. The outline of her dreams blurring away with every year. Fading until the image was almost too far gone to see.

Lying on the ground, she saw into her heart and knew that the dreams weren't gone. But they were too big for the life she had constructed.

'We need to make some changes,' she told herself. 'First thing tomorrow, we'll resign.'

Knowing that speaking to herself in third person was a sign of madness, she concentrated on the feeling of Otherness. She wasn't speaking only to herself, she hoped. She was speaking to a long line of dreams, hopes, desires, and a tree. She threw that last one in just to be on the safe side.

'I wish I'd been more daring.'

Bravery hadn't been a notion that was rewarded in her house. Her father had been big on conformity and her mother had agreed. They had existed in their lives, making sure they hadn't rocked any boats. They had walked the path side by side and when they passed, there wasn't even a rustle of leaves to show they had come that way.

'I want to make sure I leave a mark,' she told herself firmly.

Not a large one, to be sure. For even though she had come face-to-face with the idea she wasn't ordinary, a lifetime's habit of thinking small didn't just vanish overnight.

But she wanted her footprints to be noted. For someone or many ones, to note that she had been a part of their lives. Not just a random friend who listened, but one they had needed.

Something inside twisted. A sour note. She raised her eyebrow, interrogating herself.

'Not needed, then?'

The answer whispered like an echo through her body.

'The best gift you can give anyone is the gift of not needing you, of complete and utter independence. If they choose to take this independence and come along on your journey with you, all well and good, but needing to have you by their side to be able to take the next step... that is your Ego speaking.'

She tasted the unfamiliar word. Ego. Oh, she knew everyone had one. It was what made men strut and women preen. Wasn't it? She hadn't given much thought to her own. She had always believed she didn't have one. No one who wore the same trouser suits every day, had the same hair cut for years and never wore makeup, could possibly have an ego.

The leaves of the tree fluttered above her. She had a feeling it was laughing at her.

'Everyone has an ego. It tells you how marvellous you are; how self sacrificing and how much people need you in their lives to survive. It also is the thing that keeps your magnificence in check. It tells you the things you can't do. What you are hopeless at and how you'd better not step out of your small world, because what right do you have to be happy and to shine?'

She found that very confusing. How could it tell you how marvellous you were, but at the same time be the thing that kept you small?

'If you wear the straight jacket your Ego asks you to wear, it controls your life. It will tell you how much people need you, but how pathetic you are to think you can be more in life. It is this paradox that will keep you locked into the dream of being nothing.'

Some dream, she thought. Who would dream of being nothing?

'Nearly everyone. They set goals and dreams they feel they deserve. But what is guiding their idea of what they deserve? The ego. The one thing that wishes them to stay as small as possible, so they don't realise they can be whatever they wish to be.'

'That doesn't make sense. Why would I dream small?'

Again, the twist in her chest: a knot of disbelief at her own naivety.

'You, who have always thought of yourself as ordinary, ask these things? You have always believed you deserved nothing more than the happiness someone else was meant to provide. You limited yourself to the confines of a life without hope and without meaning, a life that was measured by bending and meeting other people's rules and expectations. You thought of this life as the only thing that could be.'

Lying on her back, eyes closed now, she felt dizzy, as though the ground underneath her was moving in slow, lazy circles.

It was the truth she was hearing for the first time. She could see that. She had allowed the mind to control what she thought was possible. And it had sought to confine her, so she never knew how wonderful life could be.

'What do I do?' she wanted to know.

'Know how magnificent you truly are. Acknowledge the power inside and the stars that sing for you. Find your ears and listen to all the messages around you. There is magic in every single day of your life. There is a deeper truth to all that you do in this world. Find it. Seek it out and that truth will set you free.'

She felt a shiver pass along her limbs. Inside, the universe shifted and the stars wheeled through the heavens. Her eyes flickered open and a shaft of sunlight lanced into them, causing her to wince. She'd regret this abandoned posture if she got sunburnt, she thought, struggling to her feet.

The first thing she needed to do was eat. Her stomach let her know that in no uncertain terms. It growled loudly; it had been a long time since breakfast and her daydreaming had eaten away at the afternoon.

Lunch was a light salad, dressed with olive oil and mixed with tuna out of a can. She didn't feel the need to preserve flesh. She hadn't played with vegetarianism. It didn't appeal, though red meat had been off the menu since her mother had moved out. She liked the salty taste of fish as it burst in her mouth, chomped hard with strong white teeth.

If her tree expected her to give up all meats, it had another thing coming. She wasn't going to take dietary advice from a set of twigs.

As she ate, she stared out at the tree that had started it all. She needed to come from a place of love, to not believe she was crazy. She also needed to learn not to argue. Her lips quirked: had she ever argued?

Well, not really. She'd accepted all her parents had said, believing in it so much, much of it had come to pass. But in her little ways, she had argued. Not accepting being ordinary. One of her closer friends – she argued with her. Quite a bit, actually.

What if, just for once, instead of arguing, she listened to her friend? What if, she knew in her mind deep in the recesses of the dream, that her friend was speaking from a place on another path and she could let the words wash over her without taking them personally?

There was a moment of remorse. That she had never tried that with her mother. The last few times she'd spoken with her mother they had argued, a little. Or she had sat in silence and the words she wished to say had festered on her tongue, never to be said.

That festering, she realised, only served to damage her. And shouting back only served to damage them all. There had to be an in-between.

She watched the leaves on the tree blinking at her in the breeze. They seemed to be sending her Morse code.

'The in-between you are looking for can be found in the Silence,' they appeared to be saying. 'The extremes are shouting back, trying to force someone to hear your point of view while knowing all the time they never will, for they are blinded by their own point of view. Or the other extreme is sitting there wanting to wring their necks, feeling bitterness pulling you down, because they are trying to beat their ideas into your silence.

'The in-between is loving them in silence. Is allowing them to rant at you and not allowing it to change how you feel about them. Is watching what you say, so that you speak your truth at all times, but not in a way that forces them to notice if they do not wish to. That is their path. You allow their words to wash off you, holding only onto love. Believe that they have their reasons for being so angry and aggressive in asserting their will. They are afraid to hear. From a place of love, you just may find the words they have needed to hear.

'But know that their words cannot change the truth as you know it, so there is no need to argue. If all is love and you are everywhere, why would you argue with yourself?'

There was logic in there, she agreed, sipping tea. Though it was fuzzy and lined with images of psych wards.

'What about romantic love?'

She had to ask. She was still in two minds. Could she find something as elusive as love this late in the game?

She had friends, a few, who were still with the same person they fell in love with just after high school. Those lucky few who had always known, in some weird and abstract way they could never fully explain, who it was that completed them. They would look at each other and you could see the history in their eyes. The shared laughter and 'in' jokes only they knew the background to and they could never fully explain to others. The way they would reach out and the other would know and have their hand ready.

She wondered if perhaps the drive to have a great education had driven her away from the potential to have that sort of history with someone. Even if she was to meet someone now they wouldn't have shared the tumultuous twenties together. They would have differences and different friends who knew them from long ago with experiences that they couldn't share with someone new.

She found that very sad. If she hadn't been so keyed up to experiment; so concerned that she would disappoint her father by marrying too young, without a proper education under her belt, perhaps she too would have a history with someone.

Though there was a part of her that wasn't too sure if she cared. The same part of her that no longer craved the two point five children and the dog with its waving tail, shied away from the idea of being with someone from the age of nineteen, like one of her girlfriends had been.

'So, what of love? Is love between two people a part of this grander scheme you are talking about?'

'Do you want it to be?' came the whispering echo of a question.

She thumped her mug down, spilling some tea. Why oh why did her inner voice always expect her to do all the hard work of coming up with the answers? A simple yes or no wouldn't have gone astray.

'I think so. Some day. There is the chance that someone will come along and make everything okay.'

Take away that gnawing loneliness that was striking on odd nights, around three a.m.

She listened to the silence and heard the answer in her heart.

'You make everything okay by loving yourself first and then you'll find the 'someone' you are looking for if that is still what you wish for. The 'someone' who will share that history with you, and laugh at your jokes, and wonder how he could be so lucky as to find someone so amazing in life. But first, you have to rescue yourself.'

She could remember thinking that, at one time, at university. That perhaps the person behind that white picket fence with her wasn't meant to rescue her. She would do it herself. But her father had told her that was nonsense. Men always did the rescuing.

She found that slightly daunting.

'No one else can complete you. No one else can make the happiness or peace come into your life. You do it. You be your happiness, so that no one can take it away. Find the strength in your own happiness so that it cannot be blown away in the face of anger, or pain, or disappointment. You be the peace of mind and the breath of joy. You take this out into the world and show them what it means to be happy, complete and fulfilled, *all by yourself*. Then know in that moment, you are everything you have ever dreamt you could be and someone will be drawn to that energy and love.

'But don't believe that someone else has to do it for you. That way leads to compromise and to staying in a relationship from which all love has been lost. When it is struggle and pain and hurtful silences that drag on for days, what you had hoped for is lost.'

She found herself nodding her head. These were ideas she'd pondered in secret moments in the darkest recesses of her mind. But never voiced because it was against everything she had been taught to believe in.

Nurture has a lot to answer, she thought, rinsing out her mug and putting it on the sideboard to drain.

She wished she had had the courage to express all the things going on in her mind to her father. Not that he would have understood. Quite possibly he'd have arranged for her to go into therapy.

Tidying up, she wandered around the house. She was feeling a bit vague and out of her mind. But it wasn't a scary feeling, so she let it go. Over the next few days, there were decisions that needed to be made – what to do about work, was one of them.

Because no matter how strange these conversations with a tree and in her heart were, they had illuminated something in her mind. Nothing she'd come across before had felt as right to her.

Working in the office writing reports and files was killing her on some level. It didn't matter if she found her husband there or not. The balancing act between working hard, not appearing to be enjoying things too much, not appearing to be too bright but certainly not stupid – now that was madness.

There had to be another way and she was determined to find it.

The Unemployment of the body –
but finding of the Soul

Four weeks after her flu had cleared up completely, she resigned. It had taken so long because there was a history of being cautious and not wanting to rock the boat that came along with her, even with her change of heart. It didn't matter that she was listening to something new in her life. The voices of the past still floated into her consciousness all the time. The difference was she was learning to separate the two.

For four weeks, she worked hard during the day and went to seminars on working for yourself and how to plan for your retirement, and fought with the inner voice along the way. When she could flex off early, she went to banks and accountants to make sure, rationally, the next step wasn't going to bankrupt her.

The house was not only fully paid off, but her savings were very healthy. This had a lot to do with the fact she never went away on holidays and kept her spending to the minimum.

'You have to be frugal, young lady. No one wants a spendthrift. And life isn't fair, so be prepared for anything. Don't go around spending your last dollar. Put a modest amount into a charity, then put the rest away in savings. Before you know it, you'll be retiring and your husband will need the help of your retirement package to manage the family budget,' her father had said.

She smiled, as she went through bank statements and investment portfolios. He certainly wouldn't approve of her sitting up late at night on the internet, working out the best way to invest her money for the most returns. But she needed a bit of lee-way.

A return to the office fulltime forever, was out of the question. The energy zinging through her body zinged right out of it the moment she settled in behind her desk. Not that there was anything fundamentally wrong with office work, she came to the conclusion. The problem was with her.

She had never been cut out for it. There was always something inside that had screamed in protest about the lack of creativity in her life. The scream had turned into a dull and muted mutter over the years, but now she had found a way to make it roar. And silence on the inside was never going to happen again.

So she plotted and planned her way to the exit.

Once she was officially unemployed, her life became thoroughly fascinating to her.

There were moments where panic would still overcome her. Late at night, when she was wondering what the next day would bring, she would study the ceiling hidden in the dark and worry.

The next day would come along, regardless of her worry. It wouldn't require anything of her and it wouldn't provide her with anything to worry about. But that didn't stop her. She was on a new treadmill of worry and she didn't know how to get off.

'If you're worried about something, dear, then you know what to do. Face it and learn all you can about it. You are worried for a reason. There is something in the idea of whatever it is that could go wrong. So know your enemy.'

Her father's words would come through loud and clear at times like that. She would hear him explaining that all worries stemmed from a truth. A real fact of something in life that is scary.

But her heart was telling her something different.

When her worries about what was next became so loud she didn't think she'd sleep again, she went back to the tree she loved so much and sat below its waving branches.

'I'm afraid and stuck. I've taken this time off away from all distraction, but now I need to know what comes next. There has to be something more.' She didn't want to add that if there wasn't, her savings would run out, her investments would need to be cashed in and she'd starve.

She sat there quietly, watching an ant.

It was a very busy little ant. It scurried to the base of the tree and walked up it for a while, questing. Walking was a mild way of putting it, she thought to herself. The ant wasn't walking, it was dashing.

In short fits and starts, the ant would explore. It would dash to one place, sniff around, twisting its little head from side to side. Then it would dash again. It went down the tree and over the flat earth around the base. She hadn't allowed the grass to grow right up to the tree base, something she was glad of now, as she watched the ant running around the ground. She'd have lost it in grass.

There was one particular place where the ground rose up and over a subterranean root and then fell back down the other side.

The ant came to this imposing structure and paused. It quested. She watched in fascination as it made the decision as to whether or not it should attempt to climb this piece of earth, or go round. For a moment it was still. Then it made two small dashes. One to each side of its original position, to see if going around was the wisest and easiest choice. But the root was long and the ground was one long hill for the ant.

It went back to where it had started from. She was amazed. It knew exactly the position it had come from. It stopped there and computed all the information its questing had discovered.

Then it went up. It came to a place where the earth had made a very small ledge and stopped. The ant stood on its plateau and turned its head around. She watched as it decided that this wasn't far enough and kept on its path up the side of the buried root until it reached the top.

The ant didn't stop for long at the top. There was far too much to do and see. It dashed from one side of the long top ridge to the other. Whatever it could sense, it liked this. For a long time she watched as the ant didn't give up its higher ground. It appeared to dance along the ridge, as it explored every inch of the raised earth.

Eventually, however, it worked out that there wasn't any food store there that would help its nest, so it moved on. She saw it make the decision to leave its vantage point and go down the other side.

What a brave little ant, she thought. It was amazing how nature could supply all the reasoning and logic the little ant needed to keep moving, to find what it needed to survive and bring back to help the nest survive too. It would dash about and make short stops and explore to its little mind's contentment, but in the grand scheme of things, that little ant was on a mission. And nothing was going to distract it for long from fulfilling the requirements of the nest.

The greater good of the ant colony was upper most in its little insect nature.

'I wonder how it is,' she spoke aloud, simply to hear a voice, 'that the instincts of such uncivilised and basic creatures are designed for the greater good of the All, and in humans we have become so individualised, we have forgotten what it means to work for a future good of any.'

This idea took root in her mind and she settled back against her tree, to stare up through its leaves, into the clouds above.

Her heart took over the conversation and instinctively gave her the answers she was looking for.

'The ant is small but knows his place. They all have their roles and they do not challenge them. There is a connective feeling between the colony as they work together to bring about the greatest good. Watch the nature of the ant and other creatures in your universe and find your answers. They have found the answers to their worlds. Even if they are small worlds in your mind compared to your own. When you can see the patterns of creation in the smallest of creatures and the grandest designs in the worlds you ridicule, you can say you understand the power of the universe.

'The universal answers are more likely to be right where you sit, than anywhere else in your rather blinkered reality.'

Thanks for nothing, she thought to herself, smiling at the rather tart jab her Higher Consciousness had delivered.

She enjoyed her time off from what she had always considered 'real work'. There was a subtle shift in her energy levels and she enjoyed making the most out of the all the little things she hadn't done before.

Each day she would wake at five thirty, something she had never done before because as far as she was concerned, that time of the day didn't, or at least shouldn't, exist. For a few moments she would lie there, completely awake and yet comfortable not to move. Shortly, the cat would come in and demand a response. Breakfast was a boiled egg and a hot cup of tea, most of the time this would be taken in the garden, under the tree that had become her poster child of inner healing.

She would get lost under that tree. The tea would go cold and her focus would shift. Not only was she now studying ants for their instinctive knowledge of the world. The longer she sat and the more she looked, the more she could see a rhythm that had very little to do with the imposed ideas her parents had chosen to follow.

The natural world would get up as the sun hinted at the day to come. Streaks of grey would shade the world and the sky would shift from midnight blue to an indeterminate blend of night and day, as though it hadn't quite made up its mind which it really was. At this time, she would hear the rustling of bushes as birds ruffled feathers and coughed, waiting for the moment to burst into song. The world would hold its breath and then the sky would dance awake with colour and birds would dash out from under shrubs and into trees, to herald their delight of another sun. Each day they had a rather surprised note to their voices. She found this funny and every day would reprimand them.

'You are all such sillies. You know the sun will come up and the day will begin, for you welcome it every day. And yet, each time you act surprised that, indeed, it has managed to achieve this miraculous state once more.'

It was as if the birds were filled with a childlike wonder at the idea of another sun, a new sun that meant they were alive to see it! *Another whole day*, they'd say. *I wonder what we could possibly get up to.*

Then they would go get breakfast and spend the day twittering around her garden, plucking random worms, bugs or nectar from unsuspecting places.

The garden would light up and the world would begin again. There was nothing unessential in the natural world. Everything had its function. Even the singing of the birds, the magpie who had taken up residence perched in the boughs of her tree and sang to her as the sun peered over the back fence, had a purpose. His purpose, she thought, was pure joy. He was singing to let the whole world know there was nothing more grand than that morning.

Which he told the whole world every morning.

Each day was more grand, more expansive, than the next, in the eyes of her companions.

There were birds and bees, as spring flowers began their dance. There were flowers and new shoots all over the place. She hadn't been a tidy gardener and now the results were showing. There were random flowers sprouting in the lawn and vibrant colours all over the place, certainly no patterns to be found.

Then there were the insects which hovered and buzzed and nibbled their way around. Some of which were so fascinating, the cat would follow them keeping a cautious distance, watching with its tail flicking and ears pricked up.

Sometimes, she would forget to leave that place. But her stomach would remind her several hours later that while solitude and contemplation were marvellous things, so was eating.

There was a part of her that realised this couldn't go on indefinitely. But she felt as though the whole world, her limited part of it anyway, was holding its breath while she played with the idea of being either an intuitive and thus one with nature, or completely insane and in need of voluntary (or involuntary) admission into an institution.

At this time, she found her way through the city into parts she could never have visited previously.

'There are places you can't go, young lady. Places that no self respecting young woman would be seen in. They are populated by hippies, gangsters, new agers (said with utmost contempt, as though her father knew what they were) and possibly even homosexuals. You do not wish to get mixed up with that lot,' he had warned her.

Looking back, she wondered why she'd never had the courage to tell him about the woman she had slept with at university. He'd have shut up and gone grey.

It just may have been worth it.

Today, she thought, as she tightened the belt she'd bought only two days before around a sheath dress with black tights and knee length boots (daring to wear something new was the least of her problems, she considered talking to trees a far greater sign of madness than knee boots), she would go into new places. She would physically take herself off and eat in Chinatown or something like that.

She loved noodles. That was a discovery over the last month. It hadn't fit into the rather controlled and limited diet she'd always had. But noodles were now a must.

'Can't be eating that new-fangled Asian stuff. Lamb chops or beef roast was good enough for us when we were kids and it's good enough for you. Our whole generation was brought up on meat and three veg. Can't see any reason to change. You don't know what you're eating in those places. Probably the local cat population.'

She shook her head, as she drove towards Chinatown. What would her friends have thought about her family if they had ever heard her father's racist raves? It was enough to make her want to jump out of the car and run around, apologising to all the Asian people she could find.

Parking was always interesting at the best of times. Finding a place in Chinatown was a nightmare. In the end, she parked a couple of blocks away and walked.

It felt amazing. There was freedom, she realised, in just about everything you did if you were prepared to look for it. Knowing this was a place she'd longed to explore, but never had the courage to do so, and now was – was liberating. It was the little things that counted in the new reality she was paving for herself.

There were too many choices. The place was littered with restaurants and little shop fronts, in an almost obscene abundance. She was overwhelmed in moments. But instead of doing her usual thing and turning and running home, she braved out the initial panic. Eventually her heart stopped pounding like an express train, and she was able to enjoy peering into the shops and even browsing in others.

The smells were intoxicating. Her nose, so used to the same old diet for so long, was twitching in excitement. The past few weeks had been a revelation in so many ways. The opportunity to explore her keen sense of smell had been a surprise.

She'd always thought her nose was merely functional. It told her when things were off and when things were nice. Off and nice. Polar opposites and a controlled way of looking at things. There hadn't been much reason to explore a vocabulary for the nose.

But since talking to her tree and buying men's aftershave, she'd certainly started to apply new words to her nasal experience. There was a very big difference between off and nice. There were whole dictionaries of difference.

There were flowers that smelt sweet, bitter and like sunshine. There were incense sticks that burned a smoke that made her nose bubble with champagne-like delight; and rose oils that brought out a sensuality she'd never known she'd possessed.

All of this had been hiding behind meat and three veg, the desire for no change and no exploration of the wider world of taste, smell and sensation. She was glad she'd managed to find a way to open her senses, even if it had started rather bumpily with a visit to the aftershave section of the department store.

Now, she followed her nose. The sauces and spices that lingered all around her, until the air was saturated with them, provided her with a gourmet of smells. She wandered along sniffing the air, following the scent of spice until she walked right through the front door of a Thai restaurant. There, she stopped.

Time to experiment.

'Table for two?' asked the young girl, wrapped up in silk and smelling like an exotic flower.

'Ah, no. Just for one.' She stumbled over the words. Perhaps she wasn't as fiercely independent as she had thought.

It was still hard to be a number one. In a society that appeared to revel only in the concept of pairs or groups, the ones had a terrible time. Not that she thought that was a good enough reason to be with someone. No, her mind was made up. Her ideal person (man or woman, she really wasn't all that fussed, because truthfully, weren't you meant to fall in love with their insides? Then what did it matter what their outsides were like? It was just a covering; just something that clothed them and they would discard when the moment was right) would come along and all would be well.

Or they wouldn't.

She was determined not to settle for second best just because she was all on her own. Why take something that didn't 'fit' just to take away the loneliness? In the long run, she thought, it would be far *more* lonely to be in a relationship that wasn't full of fun and laughter and love, than to be on your own. She kind of liked the idea of learning to cope in all aspects of her life before she committed to someone.

Then she'd know. She'd know that she was with that person because they were wanted and loved and a part of her soul. Not because she needed them.

Need, she realised after her gentle chastisement from her tree (heart), was insidious. Those she'd spoken to felt they loved to be needed and needed to be needed. Or they needed someone else. And that person was enjoying being needed. The thing was, her heart had explained, this created a cycle of dependency that stunted both of them. Not needing anything or anyone was to be truly free. Then you would be in a position to give of yourself freely and without strings.

She remembered one of the boys a friend had dated.

The more her friend had needed him, the more the boy had puffed out his chest and pounded on it in animal delight. He'd been *essential*, her friend had explained.

He took out the garbage, changed the oil in her car, arranged their evenings out, paid for them, did her taxes, opened her car door and even offered his opinion on all her outfits. He'd been greatly needed, until he wasn't there.

The needing of him had worn him out and he'd gone elsewhere

to have his fevered brow smoothed by the tender hand of someone who didn't need him – but wanted him all the same.

The girl had collapsed; her world shattered. Her needs unmet, she'd had to start again.

All of this flashed through her head as she went to sit at the table in the Thai restaurant, on her own. She didn't need to be the other half of a two just to be a worthwhile person. There was much more to her and to her life, than the idea that someone would come along and complete her.

She was now on the way, it came to her with a jolt, of completing herself.

A smile twitched the corners of her mouth. Then with sheer abandon, she laughed out loud. Other diners gave her odd looks, but all she did was smile at them. Admittedly with a rather pink face. She hadn't lost all her inhibitions. She could almost see her mother shrinking under the table in embarrassment; it was such a clear picture in her mind.

This made her smile once more. Then she became engrossed in her menu and completely forgot to be concerned or feel out of place, being the only person there without a significant other.

In the end, she picked curry puffs, because they sounded so delicate; like puffs of smoke, and the Pad Thai because she wanted her noodles, after all.

Hours later she struggled home, exhausted and replete. She'd tasted of life. Smelled smells she'd never dreamed of, eaten food on sticks as she wandered through stalls and bought herself a Chinese lantern on yet another stick. There had been a dragon, heralded by cymbals and drums, that had run amok through the crowd in colours so bright her eyes had streamed.

Where had she been all her life?

The cat pounced on her as soon as the door opened. No one, he informed her, liked to be left alone all day with nothing to play with. On that note, he started to shred the lantern so pretty coloured paper fluttered all over the floor.

'Stop that, you wretch. I promise no more all day excursions. I can hardly walk straight.'

She put that down to exhaustion, not the sake she'd consumed in the tiny Japanese place just before coming home.

Tipping herself into bed, after feeding and mollifying the cat, her head spun slowly and joyfully in one direction, then turned around and went the other way. Her mental barriers and 'stuff' that she filled her head with every day that denied her heart's conversation and told her she needed therapy, went still. There was no place in the light-filled hollow of her mind for any negative self talk.

She could feel the cool softness of her pillow against the back of her head, and the bed cradling her body. The sheets were satin and not only cool, but silky to the touch. She tested the feeling by wiggling round. She wasn't entirely sure she liked satin, but had bought them to try anyway. There was a constant feeling as though she was about to slide right out of bed, they were that smooth. But she persevered.

After a mammoth shop the previous week, she had a crystal lamp on the dresser opposite the bed. It glowed now, softly taking the edge off the darkness. She preferred to be able to see her ceiling, as she spent a lot of her time these days staring up at it.

The crystal was rose quartz, set with a low wattage bulb embedded within. Thus, the room glowed with a pinkish hue and her heart beat in time with it.

She pondered the sensation.

She'd never thought of her crystals having a heartbeat before. But the room definitely appeared to be moving with her heartbeat and the crystal was echoing it. Sitting up made no difference, except her heart went a little faster.

Getting out of bed, she went over to the dresser and picked up one of the other crystals there and brought it back with her. It wasn't a polished stone like so many. It had bits and pieces sticking up out of it in a very jagged way. The crystal was brown and warm, and it settled into the palm of her hand and into her mind with a solidness she found disconcerting.

Without her mind interfering, as it usually did when she contemplated doing something she'd never done before, she felt free to explore the crystal. With every beat of her heart, she could feel the beat of the crystal. It was as if she'd found its centre and the heart of the matter.

She took a long time to go to sleep that night.

In the morning, things looked normal once more. Crystals were just rock and her heartbeat wasn't infecting them with a life of their own. She was determined not to drink anything ever again, because not only were mind altering things not so great for the system, she had a sneaking suspicion her crystals had taken advantage of her. So: no more weakened states. No more sharing heartbeats or whatever had gone on. She frowned at her array of crystals and made up her mind to ignore them for a couple of days.

That would teach them.

She spent the day in a bookstore. A very alternative bookstore she had discovered while walking to Chinatown. It was in 'that' part of town. The part her father had strongly objected to and the owner/operator was a very feminine man who wore beautiful pearl nail polish. It didn't bother her. He was lovely and full of knowledge.

'You found the heart of your crystals? That's fantastic! They must be ready to talk to you, if they showed you their hearts.'

He was very enthusiastic and she found herself talking about her tree and the conversations it appeared to be determined to have with her. He laughed and told her it was the voice of her heart or True Self.

'You must have been blocking the ideas that wanted to be heard and so you found another way to get the answers. When it first 'spoke' to you, were you asking lots of questions?'

She thought back to that day, and realised that it was her rational mind that was getting in the way. She hadn't learned to let it go. On the day the 'tree' or her inner self, spoke to her rational self, she'd been half under the influence of fever and infection. She'd already been hallucinating a brightness to the world and colours she'd never seen before. It had been a simple step from that to listening to a gum tree tell her what to do.

In fact, the more she spoke about it and the more she thought about it, the more she realised that it hadn't just been a simple step. It had been the most logical and obvious step she'd ever taken.

She glanced at the bookstore owner as her cheeks went a bit pink. Stating that it was logical to talk to a tree, even in this friendly environment, made the conscious her cringe. The inner her – exalted.

She told her inner voice to shut up. Logic brain was in full flight and didn't want the interference of her heart.

'It makes no sense. How can I be hearing things, whole conversations that are happening only in my head? Or in my heart,' she added to forestall him, as he'd already opened his mouth to contradict her.

He offered her a seat and put a Closed sign up in the window. Making a cup of herbal tea for them both he settled on the couch opposite.

It was a relaxed bookstore, with couches and seats and even pillows for those who wished to be really comfy.

'Everyone is connected to the universal consciousness, whether they admit it, acknowledge it, or even want it. It's there, patiently waiting to be of use to you. It guides you and brings you all that you may ask of it. Most people are constantly telling themselves that their 'story' is real and that there isn't enough of whatever – pick your poison – in their lives. So, the universe obliges. It gives them not enough.'

He sipped his tea and smiled at her over its rim. She was fascinated. He had eyes like a wolf, all silvery and intelligent. His boyfriend, she decided, if he had one, was a very lucky man. He had that inner glow to him that spoke of deep contentment, not only with himself, his place in life, but life in general.

Her palms heated up as her excitement grew. She knew she was about to get answers. There was always a place where the mentor filled in the blanks. She'd watched enough TV to know this for fact. She just wished she was the mentor.

'What exactly is the 'story'?' she asked, sipping peppermint.

'Your life: the drama of being human. You go from one event to another and you drag along with you all the thoughts and feelings and actions of previous events, like a mammoth weight at your back. A backpack full of the pages of your story. And you trot them out when asked how you are and recite all the drama of a lifetime. You become so attached to the story you forget to live for the moment you are currently in, holding the drama in front of you, like evidence.'

'Evidence of what?' She'd never had such a conversation. She realised that the small chats she'd had with her tree, or Self, if you prefer, were just the tip of the iceberg.

'Evidence of how important you are, reinforcing how right you are to think as you do about yourself and others. The insecurity of being human is that you aren't of value, that it doesn't mean anything and you go through life with no one noticing you.'

Her heart thudded uncomfortably. That sounded very similar to her old fear. The fear of being so ordinary that she would never matter to anyone, that there wasn't someone out there who thought she was special. She squirmed in her chair. He smiled. It was as though her thought could be plucked out of her head and held up for him to read.

'You don't yet realise that just by being here, you are important. That there is a place and role for you and the journey to it has begun. If everything happens for a reason, and believe me once you've started this journey you'll see that it does, do you really think you are here by accident? Talking to me by mere chance?' He leaned forward, as though creating a sense of intimacy amongst the whispers of his books.

'You don't need someone else to tell you your value. You don't require a world which is full of acquisition to tell you what is important and what you have. It's all there, on the inside.' He sat back. 'The most important person you'll ever speak to is Yourself.'

Now that sounded like the sort of mumbo-jumbo her tree had been trying to explain, but not quite as succinctly. She peered into her mug, wondering if he'd put something in the tea that wasn't just peppermint. All of this was beginning to make the sort of sense that made logic brain sweat.

He smiled in a lazy way that made her want to slap his face. It was okay for some. He'd had time to come to grips with things like universes on the inside, and talking trees and crystals with heartbeats.

She could hear, at the very edges of her senses, the books around them talking their messages to him. It was a conversation she wasn't really privy to. But the idea and the sense of it was quite an exciting one. Fancy not having to read ever again. You could just ask the book for a précis of its content.

'So you're telling me that listening to a tree is as good as hearing myself think?'

Was it really that simple?

'Sort of... it's just not the conscious you're used to talking with.'

'Hold on a second. You're making me sound crazy,' she said.

'That's what your conscious Ego brain would like you to think. That way you'll stay trapped in the cycle of fear and insecurity. You'll always ask your logic brain what to do and it'll always have a nice safe answer to tell you.'

That didn't sound too bad.

'But the trap is it isn't the best answer. The best answer comes from the inner stillness you find in silence and communion with your inner Self. It doesn't have an agenda, like Ego does. It just wants you to experience everything you can possibly be. So it sits back and lets that happen. But it's delighted when you ask for its help. So delighted, in fact, it'll never shut up once you've found a way for it to communicate with you.'

'Tell me about it,' she said. There were moments of silence. But anytime she thought about something, her inner voice would come up with an answer. It was as though someone had thrown a switch and now she was 'on' all the time.

One of those moments of silence enveloped them now and she could feel the shifting in her heart, as though Ego was finally submitted its will to Soul. It stretched out, thin and quiet around them, then he continued.

'The best thing to do is just relax and enjoy the ride. There is no harm in listening to what your subconscious has to say. Unless you think you need to go out and become a mass murderer. I would definitely advise you to come back here and have a chat before you do that. Otherwise, go. Enjoy. Listen to what you really want to do. All our lives we're told what to do, what will be best for us and how to do things. Now is the time for you to listen to something other than society.'

'The trouble with that is I still have to live *within* society. I can't exactly go around pretending the rules don't exist, because they do and I have to live within them. I still have to pay the bills and eat food to survive.' She was a bit fed up with the whole New Ager ideal of living life as though it wasn't reality. That wasn't going to put bread and butter on the table. It certainly wasn't going to pay for her to live.

'I'm not saying step off the planet. We've all chosen to come here for some reason or another. I'm just saying, within the constraints of what you perceive of as 'society', do your own thing. Once you begin to realise that freedom is mostly on the inside anyway, you'll find there is very little you can't do.'

She looked closely at him and then around the store. It wasn't as though he was making waves. He sold books. He sold a lot of esoteric books on many subjects from string theory, crystals and universal energy to Meditation for the very beginner. There wasn't anything in the store that would cause a riot.

He watched her interest in the merchandise.

'I don't feel I'm restricted,' he told her. 'I explored all the avenues of my heart, meditated a lot and came to the conclusion that I am not a Messenger. I am not here to create a message for others, or to be of any earth shattering service. I found my love, my passion, was books. I love everything about them: the way they smell, feel and the messages contained within them. This, then, was to be my little service. I would gather together books from all spiritual messengers and theorists, and create a place where people could come and find them. When you find what it is you love to do, you practically shine with the passion of it. You may not think you are doing much, but you are shining your light in the world and that lights up the darkness in other people's hearts. They think to themselves – I wonder what he is doing with himself? He's always so happy, peaceful and content. So, I found my love and now I'm happy.'

It definitely had a good feel about it, she conceded. The whole store glowed softly with down lights through to the back. While at the front a massive bay window complete with window seat invitingly sprinkled with coloured pillows, provided natural light.

The books had nothing to do with conventional religion. She was curious about that.

'Religion,' he said with patience, but she could also detect some horror, 'has little to do with spirituality. Spirituality is a journey for the Soul that is personal and private and goes into the universe within. I have found religions to be loud and expressive, and all about the Outside. To me, they tend to be oppressive and dictatorial. Claiming to love one another and preaching forgiveness, but all about demanding that you believe in them alone, or you're going to go to Hell. A man-made concept to keep the masses in line.

'They have instigated wars, killing millions in the name of God, and not seen the irony of it all. They have refused to bury people in so called consecrated ground if they have been perceived as sinners; instead of forgiving everyone all sins. The Master, Jesus, spoke of forgiveness and love. These things are quiet and simple emotions. But religion is about show and tell. It's not for me.'

She broke in. This was an interesting topic and she wanted to explore it some more.

'You talk about sin. Do you believe in it?'

She could almost hear her mother and father drawing breath, as though to explode. Sin was what transformed your life, they had taught her to conclude, not love. The fear of doing something wrong, the fear of going to Hell, the fear of God not loving you because you sinned, these things were the things that kept a whole generation or more, under control. Not the concept of all unconditional love and compassion and forgiveness.

'Believe in sin? No. That I do not. There is no evil, no sin, no negative energy and no evil spirits which can take your Soul away. Why would an all powerful, Almighty God create such a thing? A God of love and compassion wouldn't. It is obscene to think that there is an equal and opposite force. Because that would defy the fact that He is *all mighty*. He'd only be half mighty or partially mighty or even *shared* mighty, if there were an equal. No, it is like the bogeyman under the bed. We have created a shadow because there is power to religion if there is a reason to be afraid. But there is no reason to be afraid. No reason to beg for forgiveness. You are forgiven the moment you are born, for there is nothing you do that is so terrible God's love cannot overcome. And that is all based on the idea that somehow, somewhere, we got separated from God, that we are not a part *of* Him, It, the Universe, whatever you wish to call the Power of Love, but somehow, apart *from* It, which I don't believe at all, quite the opposite, in fact. If you are finding the answers *inside* and the universe responds to all you think and do, then how can we be apart from *anything*? It means we are all One, we are all, in my opinion, The One.'

Inside, she could feel the sun come out. She knew there'd been a lingering attachment to those Sundays where the man in the pulpit had breathed fire on them all and spoke of a God who smote the non-believers with the eternal fires of Hell. As the man in front of her spoke, a sense of peace echoed through her heart.

She had nothing to fear. There was no reason to wake sweating at three in the morning. There was more than enough love to go around and she wasn't missing out on any. The whole world was full of it. Just waiting for people to open their hearts, use it, and expand.

'It doesn't run out?' she whispered.

'That's right,' he said, not even needing to clarify what she was talking about. 'It never runs out. The love goes on forever and keeps growing, the more you use it. It's called the big bang theory. If the scientists can agree on the fact that the physical universe is always expanding, why can't love? Why can't the one emotion, one feeling, one constant in the universe keep on expanding for eternity? If you carry the universe within you, the creative energy of life, there is always the possibility it keeps expanding on the *inside*, just as it does, on the out.'

She stood up. It was time to go. He'd helped her and given her much to think on. Inside, she was feeling overwhelmed.

'Just remember,' he said, shaking her hand and holding open the door, 'it may sound complex, we are talking about a whole universe here after all, but on the other side, it is very simple. Love grows. Do what you love and you'll grow. Evil is the bogeyman in the closet and while the shadows of humanity like lust, greed, pride, and a distinct lack of compassion, may seem to rule so much of our lives, there is the chance in all situations to allow our inner strength to be greater than the fear. After all, growing and changing are the only constants in the world.'

On that note, she found herself on the pavement, the door closed firmly behind her. Wandering back down the street, her head was spinning. There was so much to take in. The ground seemed to dip and sway with the thoughts in her head.

She understood nothing, was her conclusion. With hope that there was a handbook on the weird and wacky, she'd planned to come home at the end of the day with the knowledge of what to do next singing in her head. Instead, she just put the kettle on and crept outside to sit under her tree.

If ever there was a need to feel the cocooning love of an elemental like the gum tree, now was it.

'Does everything we know need to be turned on its head before we understand what is happening in our lives and go forward to the next step?' she asked.

'What makes you think there is a next step, or that you have ever understood anything at all?' came the response. 'You do not need to know the how or the why of everything in the universe. All you need to do is be love and be joyful and be patient. Above all else, be patient. Be true to yourself and find what it is you love to do in each and every moment.'

'That's the next step I keep talking about!' she practically growled in frustration. She didn't mean how to put one foot in front of the other. She had that bit down pat. It was the knowing what it was that she was passionate about and what she could do about it and how to weave that into her whole life, that she feared she was failing at.

She bit her lip. She couldn't believe that she really didn't know what she was passionate about.

'How can I not know what I love?' she whispered.

'Simple,' the breeze whispered back.

'All your life you have been told what to think, from school, from home, from work, the media and the world. You were told what was best for you – a good education and to work hard. You were told what to do, when to do it and what you should want, including a home, a husband and a family. Nowhere in there were you *asked* what you wanted, what you liked to do, what you thought or what you loved. It was assumed. It was all laid down by the generations before you and the walls of your society. But no matter how well meaning people are, no one can really know what is best for you – except you.

'You've had no experience in deciding. Most of the world has no experience in truly finding what it is their heart bleeds for, aches and yearns for. Not the superficial desires, but the solid ones underneath all that, that fill you up and make you feel whole. You've been told that owning the right car, the best phone, the new clothes, the ideal haircut, will somehow fulfil you. The world is designed to *tell* you what comes next; not allow you to discover it for yourself. It is little wonder you flounder when you realise that you need something else to be happy. You just haven't found what that something else really is and very few people can lead the way, as few have the courage to ignore what others tell them.

'Be gentle with yourself. Be kind. Tell yourself – *it is okay for me to be human.* The most empowering words in the human vocabulary, no matter what the language, are *I don't know.* So – say them often and be humble about the not knowing and in time, you'll know it all.'

She sat there smiling under her tree until the stars came out – inside and out.

A simple beauty

'I'm setting myself a new routine,' she informed the cat.

To make sense of what was happening in her life and to leave room inside for her to find what it was she loved, things had to change.

Routine helped her to feel comfortable. Humans could be set in their ways, which she didn't think was a bad thing. But she needed to tinker with her routine so that she could start to change lifetime habits.

'Small steps at a time.' She was enjoying chatting to the cat. It lent some sort of normalcy to her dialogues. After all, nearly everyone she'd ever met who had a cat, talked to it. Unlike her, though, most of them wouldn't expect an answer.

Such was the state of her mind, with the breathing crystals and the talking tree and answers on the breath of the wind, she half expected the cat to join in. When he merely continued washing himself, oblivious to her, she knew it wasn't the cat she'd hoped it would be. There was a lot to learn from cats. This one just wasn't sharing.

There needed to be shape to her day. The endlessness of them wouldn't last forever and she was dreading a phone call from her accountant asking for an emergency meeting. Investments weren't always rock solid and she was only in her thirties. There was the rather large chance she'd need some sort of income and when that day came upon her, she didn't want it be a nasty surprise.

So there was a plan. She looked over at the cat. It had slowly grown, as she had spent time with her tree and all her other expanding interests, from kitten to lanky cat. He still demanded time with her, but he didn't need much except a comfort pat or some food. She had ceased to think of the cat as a companion – it wasn't joining her in going forward, so she treated it like a dependent child. There was a lingering knowledge in the back of her mind that somewhere, not yet a twinkle in another cat's eye, there was her companion who would teach her all about the life of a cat. She gave her current one a disgruntled look. It wasn't going to be him.

The new regimen included many trips back to that bookstore. This time she wasn't there to demand answers from the owner, who merely smiled at her every day and let her amuse herself. She was surprised that he didn't seem to mind she never bought a book. Instead, she would set herself up in one of his squishy couches, buy a mug of his coffee (he sold the best coffee and she wondered if he charmed the beans) and settle in for some serious research.

He had laughed at her once. Mentioned something about this not being a library, but hadn't been offended. He'd shushed her stammered apology and told her that someone so raptly on a new journey needed a place to be safe to explore all options. This was that place and he'd leave her to it. His business was booming anyway, and she watched as he treated all customers, no matter what their background, with compassion and humour.

She still got up early and spent time sitting under the tree, sipping tea and planning a glorious day. The freedom of it all sometimes overwhelmed her and she got quite giddy with the headiness of it. She could see miles stretched in front of her. Miles of endless exploring in a world made to be played with.

After her morning ritual and relaxation in the garden (sometimes she'd have to wander around and make sure all the other plants were happy and well weeded), and a breakfast so light as to be non-existent, she'd pack her backpack. In would go notepad, pencils, pen, phone and her wallet. Gone were the days when she would pack her lunch. She knew it was crazy, wasting money on buying lunch when packing one would be far more frugal. But the bookstore was close to so many interesting places to eat. Her taste buds demanded she try everything her nose could smell.

She knew it would take a while.

She wasn't greedy. She didn't mind if this revolution of her tastes took the rest of her life. There were so many things she'd missed out on; she wanted to try them all. And the wonderful thing was - she could.

The world, she realised, was there to be experienced. To try out all the amazing things people had come up with. To sit there and sip an exotic tea for half an hour, savouring every mouthful because each time it landed on her tongue, she could detect something new. Or to go back to a favourite cafe or restaurant and each day have a different thing from their menu.

This was decadence.

It wasn't making millions, or travelling the world. Though she thought it would be rather nice to do this sort of exploration in somewhere exotic like Turkey or Italy.

The decadence in her life came from the slow, long experience of everything around her. Lunch went for nearly two hours. There was no need for the hurry she'd surrounded herself with in the past. The world was a smorgasbord and she was the only diner. There was wealth in every mouthful and abundance in every hour.

Then she'd be back at the bookstore, reading, and note taking, and thinking.

Her thoughts expanded with her world and she would write for the remainder of the afternoon, allowing the free flow of thought to pour out of her. She was sure that somewhere in these sessions finding new material in the bookstore, writing about it, or sitting eating lunch, holding the tastes in her mouth for as long as she could, she would find the love the tree had told her about. The kind of love for herself, for her passions, that would show her the Next Step.

Not only would she spend many hours in the bookstore, but she would go to workshops and group discussions in the strangest of places. Determined not to close her mind to anything, she ended up feeling as though her brain was spilling out.

There were so many paths out there!

So much information that could set her feet upon a new direction, each leading the person who thought of it closer to a universal truth, but each was so different. She felt overwhelmed.

Eventually, she closed her notebook and left the store. She needed to be away. Far away. The bookstore owner smiled at her words of goodbye and promised she was always welcome, if indeed, she was ever to return. He suspected she would not.

Finding a loving home for the cat who wasn't a lifetime companion, she packed up her things and took a trip. She hadn't planned it and thought this was truly free-wheeling through life. She hadn't booked a single place to stay, or passage to anywhere.

The night before she took off in her little car, with its boot packed full and backseat spread with blankets, jackets, swimmers and other odds and ends, she merely closed her eyes and let her finger wander around the map of her country, her area. This wasn't the time to fly off and desert the discoveries. Now was the moment to truly find out what her backyard had to offer.

Her finger had landed on the coast. She'd never been to the coast. It wasn't in the scheme of things her father had been so determined to live by. His voice was much softer these days. It was almost as though his ideas of how she should live (exist) wasn't compatible with the things she was trying, and so he'd slowly started to go. Instead of shouting in her head, she could hear his cautions like a whisper.

It was only to take about four hours to drive to the coast. It took her seven. There were things to see on this trip she'd never been exposed to. Delights to senses she'd never realised she had.

Sights of long flat lands; bare of anything except perhaps one tree or a group of rocks. Grasses waving in the cool morning summer breeze.

As the day heated up and she headed into the hills which seemed to ring the coastline, heat shimmered through the trees. Hill country was so vastly different in nature she pulled over, locked the car, and walked out onto the land. There were no fences, so she didn't think she was trespassing. Even if she was, she didn't care.

With no farm houses or indeed, any structures at all, within moments she had lost sight of the road and felt completely alone. It may have been summer, but it wasn't school holidays, so there wasn't much traffic on the road to the coast. People were at work, at school – all bound up with rules and regulations.

She suddenly realised what the man in the bookstore meant. She was still part of the world. Still part of all those rules, but they no longer applied. They didn't matter here, where naked feet squished into the rich loamy soil.

There were no rules or regulations to prevent her from doing exactly what she wished. This then was the freedom within the society he'd talked about. Finding moments within all the humdrum that spoke to her heart where no one else's ideas could touch her. This was one of those moments.

She removed her light jacket; needed when she'd left the city because the summer air had clung to the cool of the night. But now it was far too hot and heavy. She hung it on a tree branch and kept moving.

Along her path she hung different parts of herself – a jacket here, a shirt there - the parts that gave clues to her identity and her place in society. Because they didn't matter out here and there was no one to care.

By the time she reached a small clearing where a trickle of a stream danced over rocks, she was clad only in her bra and knickers. She knew she couldn't get lost, as the way back was spread with markers of her world and she could gather them up and become herself again along the way.

Dipping her loamy toes into the stream, she sat peacefully on a rock and allowed the birdsong to echo around her. She hadn't reached the mountains yet, but already the difference was palpable. There was a freshness to the heat, a clearness that wasn't available in the heart of a city. Even the water, though barely a trickle, was clear and she could see the sunlight picking out rocks underneath.

Though the temperature was climbing, she could feel the edges of a cool breeze starting to pick up, as though the trees were pushing cool air ahead of the stillness. It was so light as to almost not be there. But it was hinted at in the rustle of leaves and the strokes of feather-light coolness on her heated skin.

There was barely any sound. Just a few leaves, a few birds and the trickle, trickle of the water. She closed her eyes and allowed the sounds of the world to take away the beating of the city that echoed in her ears.

Long moments of nothing entered her being. Sensation rushed along her spine, pulling energy from the water; the very ground she sat upon. It drifted up her bones and she felt each knobbly vertebra like fibrous matter that bent and swayed with the beat of the world.

Her senses tickled her and a smile twitched her lips. Was there really anything more amazing than sitting with ones feet in cool water that gurgled along while the world breathed in one's ear, she wondered? Had she ever really slowed down enough to embrace the idea that the world was trying to tell her something? Something enormous?

She thought about the ant and the tree; the crystals with their heartbeats and the world breathing beneath her bottom and feet. There was something so natural and real and solid about them. It was reassuring her, affirming her new choices.

Her eyes flew open and she laughed out loud.

'That's what's going on!'

She'd been asking a lot of questions. Mainly because she'd been feeling so distracted and distanced from the life she'd had planned out by her father and mother. The worthy job, the worthy man, the balancing act between ambition and needing someone to fulfil her life. She'd been unhappy, without fully realising it.

It had come with a vague feeling under her skin, like itchiness when there wasn't anything there. Distraction, when she needed to focus her attention. A malaise when she wasn't unwell – a deep wondering why she couldn't find the laughter and contentment people spoke of that she witnessed in some of her colleagues. At some level, she'd been wondering what was wrong with her and if there was some fundamental flaw going on she had yet to find.

That had led to the questioning.

She grinned and wiggled her toes. Her body had succumbed to the flu which had surprised her at the time, because she was never sick. But it hadn't been about the flu. One hand lowered and her fingers traced fine patterns in the water.

It had never been about the flu.

She'd thrown off the idea that what others told her was the truth and started down the path to her own Truth. She liked what she saw, even if it was unfamiliar and rather scary.

Looking around, she had to agree with herself. It was rather startling.

Here she was, nearly naked, in some farmer's overgrown forest-like field, playing with the creek. No one knew where she was, she couldn't see any signs of habitation and the only sound that reached her came from things she'd always considered to be neither alive, nor dead. Just there; nothing more than props for the 'doing' of life. Like the breeze and the water.

She peered into the little stream and saw rocks, smoothed by years of having water rushing across their surfaces. How could she have ever thought a creek wasn't alive? There was such movement and presence inside the bonds of its water; it was practically dancing for her.

Everything all around her was reassuring her: this is Life, drink it in.

For a long moment she stared into the water, then she stood and moved away. It was getting late and she still had some driving to do. There would be plenty of water where she was headed, an endless horizon of it.

As she moved back to the car, she picked up pieces of herself, layering her body with the trappings of civilisation. As each piece settled around her body, constricting and defining it, she felt heavier, and more real, and somehow more solid than before.

By the time she reached the car, she was determined that this would be the last time she wore denim jeans ever again. The waistband had become a belt of fire, cutting her in half, moulding her legs to the uniform of straightness and conformity. While never chubby, she felt bloated on humanity.

The Tides of Life

The beach was everything, and far more, than she had ever expected. She'd seen photos and movies and all kinds of ads for the sea and the resorts that seemed to spring up along beaches like goose pimples on cold days.

But actually being there, and seeing and feeling things for herself completely blew her away.

There were sights and sounds and smells that couldn't be shown in even the best of movies. Gulls screeched overheard causing her to wince and duck, laughing as she did so. Waves crashed ceaselessly onto the shore, breathing with the world, heaving its sides in and out.

The smell of salt and seaweed mingled with fish and chips, and humanity. There was nothing new about that. People smelt of bodies, sweat and skin, wherever they roamed.

Then there was the sight of the ocean itself. The glorious expanse of water, that heaved and seethed and hissed at her from its swelling mass. It clutched at the shore, as though trying to reach everyone safely aboard dry land and tumble them into the depths. It glittered in every shade of blue, green and hinted at darker colours underneath. There was white cresting the waves, like the froth of champagne bursting out of the bottle.

She settled into a motel, cheaper than staying in one of the resorts she'd spied as she drove along the coastline. Once she'd paid her way and unpacked the myriad of things she'd jammed into the boot of the car (it is always hard to pack for an experience you'd never had before), she grabbed a bottle of sunscreen, a wide brimmed hat and walked across the road and onto the beach.

That was how close she was. How amazing, was all she could think. A few steps and then all that was between her toes were fine grains of bright white sand, right out of the photos she'd seen. It felt remarkable and so different to the loamy soil she'd walked through earlier that day.

Wiggling her toes every step she took, she found a spot unoccupied and spread her brightly coloured towel over a patch of sand. It wasn't school holidays and it wasn't a weekend, and yet there were still many bathers running and walking around, plunging frantically into the foaming water.

Many were older, holding tight to large hats and going in only up to their knees. They weren't going to allow the waves to steal them away. The others were mothers and their toddlers, a few older kids who thought skipping school was a wonderful idea, and a few others, wandering aimlessly, as they contemplated what was happening in their worlds.

Dumping everything in one place in a higgly-piggly pile, she stripped off her life once more and took a stroll. This time, she was more acceptably attired in a new bikini she'd never worn before. She wondered what made these scraps of material any more suitable than the ones she'd had on by the creek. Less material in the bikini and yet if she was caught in her underwear she'd be frowned at or censured in some way.

The contemplation of this absurd contradiction made her giggle. She was glad her walk had left the others behind and the only things to hear her laughing at herself were waves and tiny sand crabs, which dug themselves into holes as she passed. There was the thought in the back of her mind that perhaps she *was* going a little crazy – and the last thing she needed was someone coming upon her laughing at the thoughts in her head.

She found a secluded place surrounded by wet, glistening rocks and sat, staring out at the sea. The tip of the rock mass she was perched on jutted out into the water and she felt surrounded by the seething, whispering waves in a three sixty panorama. It was possible she was soon to discover, to lose oneself in the motion of the sea for hours. Luckily she'd come prepared.

Later that night, after eating a seafood banquet of crab and lobster and baby octopus marinated in something that made her taste buds blush in abandoned joy, she curled up in the motel room and listened to what the waves had to say as they murmured along the shoreline across the road. They beckoned to her, whispering that all the knowledge of the world awaited her, if only she'd let herself come play. Eventually, finding no sleep, she got dressed again and slipped out into the moonlight.

Oh, how different things were when seen lit only by the cold starlight and brilliant moon. They glittered in the sky against the inky backdrop and seemed to slide into her heart. For one breathtaking moment she felt disconnected with the solidity beneath her feet, and felt the stars scatter within.

'I'm losing my mind,' she murmured, as she sat abruptly on the wet sand, fingers of waves soaking her pants and the edges of her t-shirt.

The universe whirled around her, showing her the stars reflected in the water and shining in the heavens. She could see them all surrounding her, above and below. Instead of closing her eyes, as she normally did when meditating, she widened them as far as they would go, to take in as much of the starlight as she could.

It flowed down through the evening air and settled into her eyes and her hair and along her skin. Her pale skin, that refused to tan no matter what she did, glowed softly in the light. Here, in the light of only the moon and the stars, her skin was beautiful. Nature showed her what harsh fluorescent lights never could – she was crafted from perfection.

The porcelain of her skin kept her enthralled. She waved her hand in front of her face, wiggling the fingers one by one. They moved through the air thick with starlight, like thin, delicate slivers of silver. Her whole arm was a marvel. There was no part of her that wasn't shown to her as shining, brilliant and – dare she think it – beautiful and extraordinary.

The waves seemed to catch her delight and kicked up, spraying the world with white foam.

'See?' they whispered. 'See how amazing you are? You are made from the same stuff as us, the same power and the same energy. You are a miracle. All the things you see every day of your life are a miracle. Feel it and feel us. We are all One.'

She knelt in the salty water, as it rushed in and out in deep contented breaths. Her hands filled with the froth and bubbles that came from many miles away, from another shore, another country. The sea, she fantasised, held the world together. It linked landmasses from all over the globe and touched hands and feet with people she'd never know.

It took the power and energy from one place and deposited it, like so much flotsam and jetsam, far away.

Gathering the water, clutching foam, she went deeper. Kneeling, she was doused in cool water, from head to toe. She was barely in up to her knees if she'd been standing, but from her current perspective the waves towered over her and submerged her as they went past.

She didn't go back to her room that night. Instead, she spent the entire night walking the beach, or sitting on the rocks, or playing in the shallowest waves. And come the morning, instead of feeling exhausted, she felt more invigorated than she'd ever felt before.

Energy pumped through her body, flooding her senses. She could smell and taste and see so much more than she had ever before.

She didn't stay long. There was no need. Instead of going home, as she had suspected she might, she took a long trip.

She felt liberated. For the first time ever, she was constrained by nothing and no one. There was no parent to go home to. Her mother wasn't waiting for her to visit the retirement home. There was no voice in the back of her head telling her she was being irresponsible.

There was just time. Free time; all to herself.

There was nothing like coming home, after being gone for a long time. There is a sense of having found yourself once more, she thought, as she dropped her bags in the hall.

It was all well and good to go floating around the place, but that didn't ground her, and didn't give her the sense of being that came with the connection she had with her home. At least, she'd always thought so.

She wandered the halls and opened all the doors. The house had a stale, unloved feeling about it. She'd been gone for six months. There had been a rash of phone calls, to redirect mail to a mate's place and to alert the security firm; then more freedom than she'd ever known.

Taking a deep breath, she wondered what the trouble was. There was an itchy feeling under her skin. As though her skin was a fraction too tight and the insides had no place to go and no room to move. She kept walking around her home and out through the back into the yard.

Settling beneath her tree, she opened her eyes and looked up through its boughs and waited. No matter how dislocated she felt, there was hope the tree would ground her into place and make her feel a part of this world again.

She waited beneath her tree and sighed, as the silence grew. Perhaps, she considered, she'd been gone so long the magic had worn away. There was no spirit of a tree; there was nothing left bar the solid trunk and its leaves. Whatever had been there before was gone.

Closing her eyes, she drifted into a deep trance-like state. Images of her travels, up and down the coast, through small towns that spoke of wild nights and whispers of magic; to large cities, where all magic had fled and the dull roar of humanity blocked out the silence within.

She'd gone to see what else was out there. To see if there was something more to the life she had agreed to inhabit that she was missing out on. The conclusion was; there was a lot of confusion out there. There were many people running around, shouting at the top of their lungs 'look at me, look at me,' or, desperate not to be found they cried 'look over there, look over there'.

The clutter in the in-between spaces clogged the silence and her inner world had collapsed. The roads didn't speak to her; the highways merely shrugged her off. The waves stopped calling her name and bringing her the wonders of the far distant world; and in the cities, she no longer heard the call of a bird.

But she had discovered one important thing. Something she kept treasured in her mind, clasped tightly to her soul. It glittered among the debris of her travels, shining and growing as she now turned her attention to it. As it grew, so too did her awareness of the tree she rested upon.

It was there, all of it, just waiting for her to find the time to be silent.

'When in silence, the passion of your heart, the power of your Soul, can be found. When in silence, there is no secret of the universe you cannot unravel. When in silence, I am Here, where in fact, I've always been.'

She smiled, leaning there with her eyes closed as she studied the glittering within. Oh, she had lost some connections. She had found the tedium of travel ripped her away from her calm world of union with nature. But she had found something far rarer along the way. Because along the way, she'd found a new voice. Discovered that when the silence inside was disrupted, and she had no place to talk to Herself, there was another way.

She pulled out the notebook she'd kept by her side the whole way. It was never far from her and the pencil she carried tucked into her pocket was always sharp.

This notebook was new. There were six of them in her bags, one for each month. They were full. Full of words, images, voices and colourful characters that battered at each other in the race to be heard. Oh, she'd lost a silence. But in the previous silence of her mind, there had come a voice that had expanded and taken root, and now filled her up.

She had found a passion. A love that went beyond anything she'd been told to care about.

There were notes on books, notes on characters, and a whole novel waiting in her bag to be unpacked and explored.

In the bellow of humanity, in the untidiness of travel and the smallness of her silent time, she had found a new voice.

And it roared.

She leaned back and lifted her pencil. There were a few things she needed to add to the last part of the second volume. Then it was done. She wondered if her friend, a publishing assistant editor, would enjoy reading them as much as she had loved writing them.

In the end, though, it didn't matter if her friend did or did not like them – what mattered was the chance to touch someone else's life through the words she had written. There was nothing in the world that could compare to the feeling of having created what filled the notebooks.

Creation, she wrote, is something we are born to do: to create, to explore and create again, to live on the knife's edge of desire and create all that we wish in this world. To *show* what we believe in, to *live* what we create to be true. To see the world through the window of pure creation and know that in the blink of an eye, in the smallest of seconds, we can create it again.

So choose. Choose what it is you love the most, and put passion behind it that moves mountains. And know that what you can believe to be true; you can in fact, create to be Truth.

She put the pencil down and folded the front of the notebook closed. That was enough for one day. It had been a huge week. Travelling back, after getting an urgent sense that she was needed back home. She glanced around. It looked different, smaller, somehow.

It was almost time to make the leap. And she'd found the place to do it.

Coming back, she'd entered the city from another direction. One she had never been before. It was there she had seen it. The place she knew for a certainty would become her home. The place she was destined to love and roost in. She smiled at the thought.

It was on the edge of the city, on a large block with a lone gum tree standing tall and straight, proud in the backyard. She could easily see it over the rooftops. The house wasn't all that impressive; it had been an open day, so she'd pulled over and wandered through. But there were two things that pulled at her. Standing on the back step, she could see the hills marching into the horizon; sentinels guarding the way out. And for a moment, she could see the extension she was determined to build – wrapping around the house, with bay windows allowing all of nature to shine inside.

The other thing was the arch from living room into a small study. It flung itself over the doorway, as though proclaiming 'come on *in*, I am *delighted* to show you around'. The small room that sat off to the side of the living room looked out over the street, so she would always be able to see who was coming and what the world around her was up to. It also allowed her to see glimpses of the backyard and the base of that magnificent tree.

Considering the amount of writing she had been doing on the trip, ever since the waves had beckoned her out in the night, and she'd found the beauty that was her, she'd wanted a place for all that was inside. She could see a desk and a computer settled in the corner, with her chair able to swivel round so she could peer out of the newly created window (there was a window already there, but it was a sad affair that was neither full length, nor expansive and she felt rather sorry for it. It looked like it couldn't decide if it was a window or a porthole).

She'd taken the details of the agent and agreed to come in later that week. That took her by surprise. She wasn't usually quite so quick with her decisions. But since making that one snap decision to go away and enjoy a life time of holidays all in one, she wondered if perhaps she was going to be jumping to new ideas left and right. She grinned.

Now, at home and realising it no longer felt remotely like home, she hoped that any leftover energy from her father wouldn't bother the tenants - because, while she was determined never to live there again, she wasn't going to sell. It was fully paid off and perfect for renting out.

'Bet you would hate the idea of total strangers running up and down your halls, wouldn't you, Dad?' she asked, as she went back inside. He'd rather see the place burned to the ground than put in tenants. But there was no place for her here. And she was excited about the next stage.

One thing floats away another thing takes it place, she thought. Just like the waves and all the tides that came and went over the millennia, things in her life were moving and being exchanged. The energy firing through her had no place in the old house. The new energy was too ... big, she decided. She felt too large to be enshrouded in the narrow minded, straight jacket of constrictions and rules that had guided her life before.

It was a huge relief, then, when the place she loved had no other offers and she got it for a song. It was a buyers' market and the place did need a bit of maintenance, which she was going to enjoy doing.

At the same time, packing the old house up made her feel a bit nostalgic. After the last box was placed in the truck, she went out into the backyard and sat beneath her tree.

She knew there was a new stage in life about to be entered into. Things were changing so rapidly. For starters, she'd taken her writings into her friend, who had loved them so much they were already in the contract stage.

'They are a breath of fresh air,' the editor said. 'Let's get them ready for a Christmas release.'

Things could move when they had to.

She was back to finding her silence, which was strange, because she was still in a city. Only, it was her city. She knew much of it and slowly, she knew, she'd grow to know more. She no longer had the fears deeply seeded from childhood. Whatever would happen would happen. No matter where she was in life or on the planet. So she accepted that and roamed wild throughout the city.

Now, she curled up under the gum tree where she'd sat naked after the flu. If it hadn't been for that tree, she doubted she'd have had the courage to go out and explore, let alone quit her job and make radical changes in her life.

'Thank you,' she murmured to the leaves that brushed her cheek and whispered sweet stories in her ear. 'Thank you for speaking with me and taking the time to bother with someone like me.'

She felt a little sad and strange, thanking the tree for taking the time out of its day to bother with her. After all, what else was it going to do? It was sort of stuck in one place.

'I'm never stuck,' came the answer. And she had to smile. No matter what happened in her life from here on in, nothing would be as strange as having a tree know the very essence of what you were thinking to yourself.

'I am connected to all things. My roots go deep into the earth and the roots of everything else that ever grew, and will ever grow, tell me stories of what you do and where you go, and tales of wild untamed places, and my roots can smell the thick heavy soil of ancient times.

'My branches stretch up, so far above your head as to see you as a little fragile creature so far away. They look up and see the sun that shines on all things and the rays come down and tell me stories of far off lands, where the sun shines every day and the sands scour the earth. They tell me of times so far gone you have forgotten them and of the people who walked this land, blessing everything they met and honouring the beasts and the plants.

'I stand connected to all things. And I stand in the knowledge of this in the complete awareness that eludes you and so many of your brothers and sisters. Do not pity me my stationary state. No, rather go out and find your connectedness with all things and take me with you, wherever you may roam.'

She sat there feeling remarkably humble in the presence of such awesome power and awareness. It was wisdom, she realised; and bowed her head.

Perhaps, she had to concede, there was far more to what the Self had to say than she first thought. If indeed what she was hearing was the highest version of her inner wisdom, then what the tree was actually saying was:

'*You* are connected to all things and *you* can hear the sunlight tell you of days gone by or feel the power of the ancient soils, if only you were *aware* of it.'

There was a pause. Then the leaves upon her rustled like silver laughter.

'You found and held the silence in the roar of humanity. You found your voice in the silence of life and learned to know what it is that is in your heart. You hear the echo of the ages in all that is around you. Know that this, *this* is Knowledge. In all that is created in your Now, are echoes of the thoughts and creations of the past. What you go forward to do now is create the future. Your Self knows of all things and can tell you the riddles of life, if you are prepared to listen. You are connected to the greatest power in the universe through all things and the All of Things is connected to you. Know this then, as Truth. You are a creator and a child of the universe. There are worlds within worlds and within you, you are yet to discover. And every moment of silence that you can find, allows for a different voice to be heard and brings to you the simple truths of Life.

'In the Silence, there are echoes of your Self.'

She didn't leave the base of that tree until the sun had sunk beyond the horizon and her skin was once again a pale beauty beyond compare.

To have a life worth the living

So she wrote. A lifetime of writing, all of it bound up with the inspiration she carried around with her every day that she called Tree. Every time the words would stop and she would pause, she looked out her new bay window and thought of Tree and wondered what the next words would be. It never failed. They would flow again as the essence of her tree, the awareness of her very self, would explain what was to happen next.

Sometimes when writing exciting stories for children, a passion she never got over, not even at ninety, she would find her characters caught in an Impossible Situation. With a laugh and a sigh, she would pick up her shawl and go out to the new gum tree where she would explain the situation and ask it to talk to all the earth and all the sky, its whole family, and find her an answer.

And sometimes she would fall asleep under this tree and wake up, refreshed and knowing, with the words of the great escape just waiting to be written.

Other times, she would seek the answers to life itself in the quiet moments of silence within. There, even years later, she would find the universe waiting for her – stars continuing their patterns in the eternal sky of her life.

As time passed, she found there were many gifts given to everyone; some people just never opened their eyes to see them. That smorgasbord of life she loved so much, not only handed out experiences and exotic tastes and wonders for people to see. It handed out gifts and miracles on a daily basis, patiently waiting for those who walked by to stop and see them. Possibly pick them up for a while and see if they 'fit'.

Every day, she saw miracles and found gifts. With the understanding that there were no coincidences and that everywhere she went, she went there because she was asked to, she found the world opened itself up and poured forth knowledge, almost babbling in the excitement of having someone listening. Everywhere she went she made sure she watched the world as it went by and was amazed at the talent and the wisdom and the resourcefulness of the people she met.

Each morning, she would find that place of silence and ask what she was meant to do that day. She never stepped back from what was asked of her and at the end of each day, she could look back and see the steps of her life that had led her to this moment - whatever moment it happened to be.

The more she loved the idea of living with this silent partner, the less she ventured out into the hustle and bustle of the world. People who could see what she was, and how she loved through her words, came to her. They sought her out and she never once turned them away. Because why would she? They were no threat to her.

Her father's words were still somewhere in her head: 'Everyone is out for themselves. No matter what they say and what they may look like, underneath, there is one thing that is guiding them, and that's self interest. You be very careful of yourself and your money. They'll con you out of it all, if they can.'

There were still faint murmurs left over from listening to him, but she found peace in telling him things were not like that in her life. His experiences had coloured his life. When he went looking for the worst in people; their depravity, their untrustworthiness and slyness – he inevitably found them.

She looked into the crevices and the nooks and the tiny spaces of her city to find the joys, the inspirations and the wonders of many lives holding onto hope and miracles. She went looking for the amazement and the spirit of humanity – and inevitably she found it.

The marvel of the man who hadn't walked for fifteen years teaching himself to do so because he wanted to walk his daughter down the aisle on her wedding day; the beauty in a rainy day, where every cloud charging across the sky spoke of raw power and thunderous applause. She found the people, little and big, who cried at joy and laughed in sorrow. And she found the people who believed that the reality they were living was the dream of yesterday; so the hope for the future was making new choices.

In all that she did and all the days that she roamed, she carried with her the awareness that nothing in this world could take her away from the ideas the tree had shared with her one bright golden spring day.

PART IV: BACK AT THE END AGAIN

Full Circle

She closed her mind to the thoughts that were pouring out. It was getting on, the sun had set and the late summer twilight was fading into midnight blue. Her fingers were cramped with the typing. Retelling of old stories, she realised, wasn't for the faint hearted. It was for those younger than her, her fingers informed her. Too many years of writing had left them feeling ill-used.

It was a blessing. She stood up and stretched her aching back. The fact she'd had so much to say and so many good things come of it. The gift life had presented to her was one that just kept giving. She could write forever and never run out of words. Inside, there was a well spring of knowledge, ideas and marvels she was yet to tap into. It was just time had run out.

She picked up Socrates and made her way into the kitchen.

The place she had come to call home wasn't all that dissimilar to the place she'd grown up in. There was a large private garden, a gum tree growing somewhere down the backyard and plants all around.

The major difference was the view. This time she had been determined not to shut nature out, given any opportunity. So she hadn't. When she'd commissioned the extension that wrapped around the house from back to front, she'd insisted on those windows she'd seen in her mind's eye the moment she walked into the place: big, bay windows that brought the outside so much closer. Even when she sat on her meditation stool and stared into her candle, it was framed by the vision of her hills and plants because the windows went from floor to ceiling.

It had been the very devil to get done. Every builder she'd had come to do a quote had some objection. It wasn't until she found the man 'just passing' through, that things clicked.

He'd been on a journey that led him to strange places. A wider horizon than hers had done. She sometimes wondered what had happened to the girl who wished to see the world and taste the exotic. After the trip to the coast back in her thirties, she had realised something so valuable she'd hardly pulled up stumps ever again, once she'd made the move to come here.

She'd realised that in fact, home was exactly where she was. No place would hold secrets to the world that she couldn't discover within. There was no great hidden repository of all the world's wisdom secreted in the Sahara, or in Tuscany or any other place, except in her mind. The exotic, the experiences she was looking for, were right in front of her. She just hadn't valued them enough.

Somewhere along the line, she couldn't even really remember when, considering her upbringing, she'd bought into the commercial idea that the more exotic the location of your last holiday; the more you knew, the wider your experience. But in her experience, she'd met many a world traveller who knew very little. Who only knew that the next adventure was just around the corner. They lived with the idea that somewhere there was something better. They kept on the treadmill of movement, hoping they never actually caught up with themselves, because they were too afraid of the silence within. The din of the world drowned out the still, small Voice that spoke of the wonders of a world, self-created.

They'd certainly seen enough TV to show them that out there were people living amazing lives on streets where the women were glamorous and the men buff giants who were loyal, caring and hard and passionate and stronger than anyone else. They carried the weight of the world on their shoulders, but came home to the one they loved with an ardour that left millions of fans breathless.

So they chased the dream and slept their lives away, not realising they weren't awake to start with. Hoping that tomorrow would be better and that their suspicion their partner was cheating was merely that – a suspicion. They didn't ask what would make them happy – they assumed that the answer lay outside of themselves, in a world that really didn't care, but they hoped would cradle their dreams anyway.

She gave up on the idea of chasing that holiday. Of posting

photos to friends about how amazing such and such a place had been, because deep inside she realised the only place she ever really wanted to go was home, to make a place in the world where she was contented, happy and safe. It was a haven and a resting place.

So in the end, she turned her whole city into that place. She knew every nook, every cranny. She loved the fact there were streets even the police thought twice about going, but she would go. Those there would greet this strange middle aged woman with concern and she would share stories.

She'd also shared the contents of her handbag more than once. But she tried not to hold that against the whole area. Bullies would be bullies, no matter what part of town they inhabited. Those at the big end of town tended to take more than just the contents of your bag.

So instead of spreading herself thin around a world that was indifferent to her very existence, she lathered herself on thickly, like butter on hot toast, in the areas around her home. She shared her stories and her truths with those who would listen and wrote about them for those who would not. If they were read at all, she was glad. She'd made a life out of writing the amazing journeys of her soul and her friends; so someone was listening.

The builder who had come to do her extension was travelling the world, not searching, but sampling. Like she had done, he discovered that the exotic and the excitement of the world was a smorgasbord, and he was determined to sample it all.

He had stayed for many months. They were lovers for most of them. There had been that sort of instant attraction that lights up two souls whenever they are in the same space. They shared space for as long as they could. But there came the day when their paths diverged and the tears came and went, as many had before.

She had taken lovers over the years. Nothing that would detract from her mission of the silence and her soul's path, but loves nonetheless. She never stinted with the love, though she never really wanted them to stay.

It was part of her life, this coming and going, then the holding back at the last moment. Not of her heart, she gave that away over and over and over again. It was holding back from the idea of 'forever', with the mental image of white picket fences caging her in and a man who'd broken her heart at university.

Loving someone and being with them somehow didn't take away

her autonomy. She had a feeling that this was her path and while she shared it on occasion, for the most part she enjoyed the quiet solitude of being alone.

Once she had faced, and let go, the feeling of failure that society seemed to foist upon people, especially women, if they stayed single and childless all the days of their lives, she never looked back. Lovers were an experience to expand her heart for a while, to give of her Self freely. But they weren't something she needed to keep around her.

When they left, she would buy herself a fragile little plant and find a place for it in her garden. She would silently name it after the departed man or woman, then allow nature to take its course. As with most relationships, the fragile plant often struggled unless she spent a lot of time nurturing it. She used this as a personal way of reminding herself that relationships as people knew them were frail things, and could wither and die so easily unless time, energy and parts of yourself were committed to keeping them alive.

In her mind's eye, she believed there was a better way to have relationships. A way that didn't speak of 'having' or 'owning' someone – but of sharing and loving and experiencing with someone until there needed to be a shift and you created something new. Too many people she'd met over the years spoke of their partners, and children, as though possessions. It made her shudder.

None of the plants died. But none of them thrived like her hardy trees and shrubs. They settled into their place, guarded and sheltered by the sturdier plants and wept beautiful colours into the scenery. She enjoyed her time with them, but always went back to the heartiest of trees – the angophora gum tree that reached for the skies and gripped the earth with such power.

She looked out at the tree, as she filled the kettle one handed, the other still filled with the purring Siamese.

'Socrates, my dearest friend, you have been a source of inspiration. How could I see my life without you?'

It was a question she had been pondering quite a bit lately. Socrates would be twenty soon and she would be ninety.

Many years ago, she had spoken to someone about the choices of the soul. That the soul had already predetermined when it wished to go 'home' and pretty much nothing you did would dissuade it. That was why she came to the conclusion, some cures worked for some people, and not for others. Because for some, the need for the cure (the dis-ease) was a note of warning, a note to change their lifestyle and outlook, not the moment to die, so the cure worked.

But for others no matter what they did, even foolproof remedies wouldn't work. They were going 'home' and nothing would stop them. This was never easy for those left behind to accept, but it happened nonetheless. And the cure was deemed worthless by their grieving families for ever after.

She had made it to thirty and once she'd stepped onto this path, this journey to see just how far she could go to find her soul, she'd made a conscious choice. When her energies ran out, she wanted to go home.

There had been such a clear message at the time about that; she never had any doubts as to when it would occur.

Her life was tidily divided into thirds.

The first third had been the hard work; the life she could have had if she hadn't spent any time with a certain tree. Once that third was over, she had made new choices, ones that took her as far from the road she'd known as she could get.

That third, she knew now, had been growth. Well, all life was growth, but it had been the figuring out part – the gaining of certain wisdoms. The inner world, if she had to name it.

Then at sixty, the final third had begun. She'd felt alive and whole and bursting with joy at the prospects, desires and passions life brought. Though she'd slowly disappeared from society, she was never far for those who knew where to find her. She would never take away her help, if it was sought. But her twilight years, as she loved to call them, had been devoted more to her garden, her closer friends and to the writings of her life.

Now so close to ninety, she could feel things starting to wind down. And she was glad.

'I didn't think I would be,' she mentioned to Socrates, who had crawled up her arm and was now being worn like a scarf, allowing her to make use of her other hand.

The cat was silent. There needed to be no words between them, Socrates understood. In life there was a moment when things become so clear, so much like crystal, it was almost painful.

'When I found that moment, Socrates my darling, I almost wept.'
The cat yowled, a soft lift to the end like a question.
'Oh, okay then, if you wish to be pedantic. I did weep. I could see

how my life had gone and where I may have been if I hadn't started to ask awkward questions. I could see that time was stretching and condensing all around me and while I felt there was a forever to get things done, there really wasn't.'

She sipped the tea and stared into the hills.

That moment had come on her sixtieth birthday. Three friends had turned up. Not many, for a whole lifetime of knowing people. But they were the important ones, and she was full of love and gladness they had come.

There was laughter and joyous discovery of what the past year had held for each. They only managed to get together once or maybe twice a year. So each moment was precious and recorded in their minds with sharp detail.

She'd been sipping champagne. The only time she ever had alcohol since her thirties was on her birthday, when these special people arrived. The bubbles frothed and burst, tasting like fragile crystal in her mouth.

There was cake, a deep rich black forest cake, with layers of cream and covered in strawberries looking like red hearts in the white cream. On these occasions, they rarely ate proper meals. They indulged in the senses.

Candles were burned, allowing scents to waft on the air and delicious foods they never ate during the year came out to play, like cakes and layered trifles and pudding. It was what they now called their 'orgy'. Each mouthful savoured with eyes closed.

Then, they would pause and share another story and laugh together.

It was what made life so precious, she had realised, opening her eyes as the champagne popped on its way down her throat.

The people you met along the way, the loves you shared, the delight in the smallest thing that made your heart burst and laughter bubble up. She looked around the table, at the others and had her Moment.

Such clarity. It clutched at her heart, seizing it with an almost painful grip. If things hadn't taken a sharp left turn at thirty, these glorious, irreverent and colourful personalities wouldn't be in her life. She felt deeply that all her choices had led to that moment; to such deep and abiding calm and contentment that nothing mattered. The people she loved, the memories they shared and the moments in time that were solely theirs, were all that was and all that would ever be. Her spaces were filled with the moments of her life, echoing through her cells like memories in dusty halls.

Life would always go on providing everyone with the chance to find these moments. It would prompt and nudge people to make the choices again and again, with their hearts and not their heads. It would ask them to stop thinking about things and worrying; and start loving and feeling. Life would offer up people on that smorgasbord; people of such light and luminosity, that their personalities would dazzle and find a way to touch lives, regardless of the shell some may have constructed around themselves.

She had looked at those women and looked at the row of fragile plants, flowering in their positions at the front of gardens, sheltered by bigger ones, and her heart had swelled to the point she feared it would exceed her chest.

No matter how she felt at different times, life hadn't let her down. She had created a haven where her friends would come and tell their truth and love their loves, without fear or ridicule. There was a far greater truth in all the world and all the universe lying in wait for people if they learned to listen to the silence and trust that what they heard in those moments between breaths was the promptings of love – voiced.

She had taken her fears and wrapped them up and shown them the door. She had told them to go on ahead and live their life without her. They had travelled ahead and seen there was in actual fact, nothing to be afraid of at all.

Her moment hadn't lasted as long as it felt. Her friends hadn't seen the expression in her eyes of panic – as she wondered if she had loved enough, in truth or as intensely as she should. She had gulped her champagne and hoped that the intensity she had allowed into her life was enough. Because life began at the edges of intensity, where desire, passion and expectancy balanced you on the knife's edge of hope.

She had loved a lot, but lately far more quietly than before. And she wondered if that quietness had robbed her of the intense drives of before. But looking around, having her moment, feeling her heart fill up, made her see – the intensity was still there, feeding her passion in all the small things, in all the small and large ways, for all the days of her life.

She had smiled at her friends and joined back into the chatter, allowing the tears that had come to fall unheeded, because her friends knew. They knew that such intense emotion needed an outlet; it was never good to bottle things up and tears were a wonderful way to let things go.

So they kept the flow of conversation bubbling around her and her cat of the time had curled up in her lap and she had realised:

There was nothing more to know or have. The balance between fear and love had unravelled and love was all that was left. She smiled into the long, fluted glass and asked for more.

All the things in her life were precious beyond measure and they were all here in her own backyard.

Listening to Echoes of her Heart

Time was, she could sit and write for hours without anything stopping her. Now, her bladder would insist that she took breaks and her fingers would gnaw with dull aches. They had spent the better part of a lifetime curled around in the typing position. Either that, or buried in soil planting her plants.

It was time for a rest. There was nothing more she felt the need to say. The laptop was shut up, the cat was content, and she'd had a final cuppa for the afternoon.

'It's done, Socrates, you'll be pleased to know. And it's my birthday tomorrow, which means Mrs Franks, possibly one or two of her crystals and Jennifer and the others will be coming over for cake.'

She loved that Jennifer would be there. Daughter of her oldest friend, who had passed away the year before, Jennifer had taken over the tradition of birthdays her mother had started.

There would be quite a crowd and for a moment she remembered what it was like to know many people. The older she had become, and the more in tune with the natural world, the less she had sought out the company of others. And so many had left, as once she had reached sixty, there were far more funerals than there were weddings or births.

But the children and grandchildren of her three companions who had come for every birthday until they could come no more, would turn up for the occasion of her ninetieth. It was to be a grand event. And she was looking forward to it. Which surprised her, because she'd given up on having people over; parties were exhausting and took so much effort to clean up after. But this was one she was determined not only to have, but to enjoy, to throw herself into, almost as a last hurrah.

She glanced down at the cat, sitting calmly on the window ledge where she'd jumped. Socrates loved the view, too.

'You'll hate it, my dear. Too many rowdy children and too many people who'll want to pat the star of my children's books.'

Socrates flicked her a look, those wide, knowing, blue eyes peering out of her sooty chocolate mask. She'd been affronted, at first. To star in something so tawdry as a *series*.

But when the series was published and the books loved by millions of children, she had relented. Perhaps, the cat had agreed, there was something charming in being the star of her own works. The cat in the books was by far the cleverest cat ever to grace a story. Socrates had agreed that if she was to be a celebrity, then being a clever one would be more than okay.

'There'll even be one or two great grandchildren. That'll certainly shock the garden. Tottering steps all over the place, I imagine. Oh well, give me something to do the day after, going around smoothing ruffled feathers.'

Or ruffled leaves, to be more precise. The little children would wander around and trample on things best left alone. She smiled at the fragile lovers bobbing their heads in the wind. They'd take a bit of a beating over the course of the day. Children had little or no time for such things. They'd not only tread on them; they'd no doubt pick them to present to mothers who would coo over the idea and blush when they met her gaze.

Not that she minded. There was always time to plant some more fragility.

Once upon a time, she had decided that living her life in three parts would suit her very much indeed. She'd arrive at ninety and throw aside her physical body as it became too difficult to manage and find herself something new to do.

She looked out over the garden, the hills and felt her heart surge with the love of it all. Once, she'd been so sure of how she was going to depart, and when. She had been sure that she'd have seen all she needed of the physical world and it would be time to move on.

Only – she'd changed her mind.

A life worth living was one where a woman had the right to change her mind. There wasn't anything else she really needed to see, exactly. But there were things she wanted to *feel*. Her heart wasn't ready to exchange the pure sensation of seeing the beauty around her and loving it with such strength it pounded in her chest – with whatever came next, no matter how wonderful she was sure it would be.

This time, *these* moments, made her feel vibrant and alive.

She let Socrates and herself out onto the lawn. She picked up her wicker basket and her clippers. Perhaps she'd pick a few flowers.

The cat preceded her down the path.

'Quite right, Socrates, you clever old thing, if I've learned nothing else, it's that you lead the way.'

And so she did.

The End

Acknowledgements

No book gets pulled together without a lot of effort from many people.

After this was written, it was then read by my test bunnies, so thanks to all of you and all your handy suggestions.

Thank you to Shane who not only finds me cover art, but arranges my covers so well.

Thanks to Richard who then lays out the cover for printing, and Thomas who typesets the 'insides'.

And lastly thank *you*.

www.ingramcontent.com/pod-product-compliance
Lightning Source LLC
Chambersburg PA
CBHW051839020726
47502CB00005B/1859